# Fairy Tales and Space Dreams

A collection of fantastical short stories written by
Jasmine Shea Townsend

*To*
*Eunice Glover,*
*Mark Dawson,*
*Rebekah Armstrong,*
*Casian Holly,*
*Gabrielle Nicole Couch,*
*Edward Glover,*
*Anthony Coca,*
*Ben Noel,*
*Dean Kissell,*
*Emily Ford,*
*Hannah Williams,*
*and Patricia Cavanaugh,*
*who helped make this dream come true.*

*And to my parents, James and Cheryl, for their unwavering support.*

# Contents

## Fairy Tales

## Space Dreams

*Fairy Tales*

# Princess Snow White

Long ago lived Queen Alannah, a benevolent queen from the Northern lands who used her magic crystal ball to bring prosperity to her people. With it, she predicted droughts to avoid famine or make amicable alliances with neighboring kingdoms. She also very much enjoyed traveling, a hobby which distracted her from her loneliness. Her travels expanded far beyond the Northern kingdoms, and this made her the wisest ruler yet. This story is a tale resulting from her most important trip.

Down and further down she ventured, into the tropics of the Southern lands. Here, with skin as white as the pearls adorning her neck, she stuck out among the Southerners' earthy rainbow of shades—cinnamon, umber, cedar, carob, onyx. Her hair fell like black silk down her back, but here, the natives' hair grew around them like halos in tight curls and was often braided into elaborate updos, else their twisted tresses hung to the smalls of their backs. The local villagers welcomed her, and she stayed for three days.

On the third day, an accident sparked a fire in one of the homes, and after the flames were calmed, the home was gone, as was the young couple who'd lived there. The villagers, however, managed to save their infant daughter, an obsidian bundle of joy with a budding tuft of white hair. Queen Alannah's heart melted when she saw the child, and she instinctively grabbed for the baby, holding the bundle tight as her heart swelled. This was the face she wanted to see every morning. The Queen decided to adopt her and sought counsel from the village leaders, asking if she could make one of their own a princess of the North. As the infant had no other family, and the life of a princess in the North would far better serve the child than the life of an orphan with nothing to her name, deliberation was swift. Though the Queen's opalescent skin and brocaded fashion were alien to the Southerners, they could hear the kindness and honesty when she spoke. Nurtured by this woman, the child would be truly loved by a good mother.

Queen Alannah jostled slightly as her caravan departed from the village, and she looked admiringly at her new daughter's frosty curls as a tiny hand grasped her index finger.

"I shall name you," the queen said, soft tears filling the corners of her eyes, "Snow White."

When the queen returned with a baby, the kingdom raised its eyebrows. Collectively, her subjects' eyes asked, *What is that?* Queen Alannah answered them in an announcement from the balcony of her castle. She stared at the confused faces of the townspeople below and smiled brightly as she held out Snow White for all to see.

Then she said, "This is Snow White. She is my child now. I shall raise her to be a proper heir."

The queen's speeches were normally met with cheers and applause. Today, it was met with silence and whispers. All the same to her, Queen Alannah returned to her chambers, cradling her baby close to her chest.

*

Twelve years later, a disease spread throughout the kingdom. Days before, Alannah had attempted to use her crystal ball to seek out the most effective medicines for her people. When it yielded no results, the Queen, unable to bear the sight of her people dying, took their sicknesses unto herself with a powerful spell. Now, as she lay on her deathbed, clutching Snow White's delicate hand, Queen Alannah's sister, Brigid, schemed. Just outside the castle walls, the kingdom mourned, though more had warmed up to the idea of a foreigner raised by their beloved queen becoming next in line to rule. This meant Brigid was now second in line to the throne. Still, she could reign as queen regent for another eight years. She had time to figure out how to do away with the child. Brigid curtsied to her fading elder sister and slipped out into the corridor. Once she was out of sight, Brigid stormed to her bedchamber, locked the door, and consulted her magic mirror.

"Mirror, mirror on the wall, oh, *how much longer* must she forestall?"

The mirror replied coolly, "Be neither impatient nor in a fright. Your elder sister dies tonight."

And Brigid smiled, for her magic mirror never lied. Then, she sat on the edge of her bed and combed her long, flaxen hair. Much comforted now, Brigid asked the mirror her daily question. "Mirror, mirror on the wall, who's the fairest of them all?"

"You, oh Brigid, are the fairest of them all." This was the magic mirror's daily answer, and once again, Brigid smiled, for her magic mirror never lied.

The next morning, Brigid found Alannah's magic crystal ball cold and cracked, never to light up again.

*

Six years passed, and every day, when Queen Brigid asked her mirror, "Who's the fairest of them all?" the mirror would reply, "You, my queen, are the fairest of them all."

But today, it replied, "You, my queen, are fair; it is true. But Snow White is even fairer than you."

Queen Brigid stumbled. Snow White? *Snow White*? She sat before her vanity, searching her own face for wrinkles or blemishes and found none. As always, her skin was smooth and fair as porcelain. Her face bore the same small, pink lips and straight, regal nose. Poets wrote page after page of her beauty. Artists worked tirelessly to capture her exquisite features on their canvases. How could some flat-nosed, thick-lipped *darkling* rank higher than her?

So, she acquired a magic comb and presented it, smiling, to the young princess as a gift. It was a turquoise comb, smooth as bone, that glittered like the sunlight on the sea.

"It will make your hair flow like silk down your lovely shoulders," she said. Then her hair would wrap itself around her delicate little neck and strangle her.

But the princess only shook her head with a polite grin. "Thank you for thinking of me, but I quite like my hair the way it is."

Two weeks later, Queen Brigid managed to get her hands on a magic cream in a crystal jar and presented to Snow White.

4

"Look what I've found! It's nothing short of a miracle how quickly it brightens one's complexion."

Again the princess only shook her head gave her aunt a polite grin. "Thank you so much for thinking of me, but I really like my skin the way it is."

Queen Brigid fought to maintain her smile. "Oh, but you know, the nobles talk. I think you'd make quite a few more friends with a little powder on your nose."

"Perhaps, I would," Snow White conceded. "But I'd rather have friends who love me as I am, as I do."

Snow White had two years until she could reign, but suddenly, Queen Brigid wasn't so sure she could wait that long to get rid of her. As the days passed, she noticed how the servant boys' stares lingered as the princess walked by. Young noble boys wrote songs for her to see her smile. Poets wrote feverishly about that smile. Queen Brigid flew to her chambers in a rage and slept fitfully.

The following morning, the queen summoned the huntsman and ordered him to take care of Snow White in the woods.

"And bring me her heart as proof," the queen added.

The huntsman reluctantly obeyed.

He led Snow White into the woods under the pretense of a hunting lesson, but once they reached a spot far enough from the citadel, she looked up at him with big eyes, shining like amber gems in the sunlight, and he could not bring himself to lift his ax. Not only had he loved Queen Alannah, he'd also grown quite fond of Princess Snow White and had looked forward to seeing her ascend to the throne.

He sighed. "This isn't a hunting lesson. The queen regent has sent me to kill you."

Snow White's face fell and her brows knitted in bewilderment. She'd always suspected Brigid never liked her, but she never thought the queen regent would go this far. Her eyes watered as she struggled to grasp everything.

"So where do I go now?" she said. "What do I do? I can't go back home."

The huntsman looked past her, squinting further into the greenery. "I may know someone willing to take you in."

The huntsman guided the softly weeping Snow White deeper into the woods and reached a cottage by dusk. When he knocked on the door, no one answered, so he let himself in, wrote a note, and left it on the dining table. After bidding Snow White farewell, he found and killed a wild boar and presented its heart to the queen. She snatched it from his hands.

"It sure took you long enough." Her gaze dropped to the heart, then up to the huntsman's face. "But the deed is done? This is Snow White's heart?"

"Snow White is gone," he said.

*

Inside the cottage, everything was small but tidy. The little dining table had been set neatly with a tablecloth and seven little white plates. Against the wall stood seven little beds in a row, all covered with clean quilts.

After traveling all day, Snow White was famished and began to eat some of the vegetables and bread from the dining table and washed it down with milk. Once her belly was full, she lay on one of the beds and fell fast asleep.

Not long after the sun had left the sky for the night, the owners of the house— seven little men—returned home from mining gold in the mountains.

The first one said, "Who has been sitting in my chair?"

The second one said, "Who has been eating from my plate?"
The third one said, "Who has been eating my bread?"
The fourth one said, "Who has been eating my vegetables?"
The fifth one said, "Who has been eating with my fork?"
The sixth one said, "Who has been drinking from my cup?"
But the seventh one didn't need to ask anything, for looking at his bed, he found Snow White sleeping soundly. He gasped, and the other six surrounded him, illuminating the corner with their candles, admiring her.
"Heavens, that child is gorgeous!" one of them cried. "But who is she?"
Another dwarf fetched the note the huntsman had left and read it aloud:
"This is Princess Snow White, and she is in danger, for an indefinite period of time. Queen Regent Brigid has ordered me to kill her. Instead, I am leaving her in your care, and it is to be a secret! I trust you all will take good care of her. She will be safe here, living quietly with you."
Imagining the kind of day this poor girl must have had, the dwarves decided it would be best to let her sleep until morning. They then went on to dine on what remained of their supper.

*

Meanwhile, Queen Brigid woke from the most restful sleep she'd had in days. How nourishing that heart had been! The royal chef had truly outdone himself the night before. Now, sure of her triumph, she drank her morning tea and asked her magic mirror, "Mirror, mirror on the wall, who's the fairest of them all?"
The mirror replied, "You, my queen, are fair; it is true. But Snow White, near the mountains, is a thousand times fairer than you."
The queen choked on her tea and dropped the teacup, shattering bits of china all over her newly polished floor. That lying, no good huntsman had deceived her! Whose heart had she eaten last night? Fuming and red hot in the face, Queen Brigid ordered the swift execution of the huntsman. If she wanted Snow White gone, perhaps she'd have to handle it herself.
She disguised herself and went down to market to buy a basket of apples for two pieces of copper. Next, when she was sure no one was looking, she ducked into a dark alley and followed a series of narrow paths until she came to a small, lonely shop on the outskirts of town. Here, she purchased a vial of poison for fifty pieces of gold. Her magic mirror had informed her that Snow White lived in a cottage near the mountains, and that was where the queen headed next.
Vibrant streaks of pink and orange stretched across the dark, twilit sky by the time Queen Brigid found her; She'd been singing in the glade near the cottage, encircled by tiny animals. The wind carried her voice, clear and cool as starlight, along the forest floor. Even the birds in trees far away craned their little necks to listen. Queen Brigid's stomach soured and twisted into knots. If she heard Snow White's singing much longer, she just might vomit the morning's breakfast.
"Excuse me, young one," croaked the queen.
Snow White stiffened. Her voice halted mid-verse, and the rabbits and deer scurried away. The birds and butterflies dispersed into the darkness, leaving the girl all alone.
"Yes?" Snow White said in a small voice.

"I'm a traveling merchant, you see, but all I have right now is this basket of apples." The queen held out the basket for Snow White to see. "They're not selling very well, as you may have guessed, but I could really use the money. Would you spare an old woman a few halfpennies for some delicious, red apples?"

Snow White gave her a sad smile. She had no coins on her, and the dwarves would still be hard at work in the mines, but she knew where they kept their money. "Oh, you poor thing. Come with me to the cottage, and I'll buy an apple."

She led the mysterious woman to the cottage and gave her a halfpenny for an apple, a kindness for which the fake merchant thanked her profusely. Then she stared, waiting. Snow White, sensing the old woman's expectant stare in the dark, stared back.

"Well," she said awkwardly, "have a good night, then, kindly merchant."

"I grew these myself, you know. It would so please me to see you try it. I'd love to see the delight it brings you," said the clever queen.

Snow White, ever one to oblige, bit into her apple. Then, she dropped like a stone to the floor.

Cackling, Queen Brigid retreated into the forest shadows and made her way home.

*

The dwarves returned from their long day of mining to find Snow White lying still in the doorway. They dropped everything and ran to her, doing everything they could to wake her, but she would not stir. They carried her to bed, but the next morning, she did not wake, and her skin was cold to the touch. Soon, the seven little men somberly prepared a glass coffin for her wake. Only they would attend her funeral, but that didn't mean she didn't deserve a proper ceremony. They engraved PRINCESS SNOW WHITE in gold letters on the case and rolled it out into the sunlight to mourn. Thus, they thought, passed the greatest beauty ever known.

A rustling in the woods startled the little men from their reverent silence, and a handsome, well-dressed young man emerged from the foliage with his horse. He stared at them. They stared at him.

"I seem," said the young man, "to have stumbled upon something. My apologies."

"I'll say," one of the dwarves said, clearly irritated.

Then, one of the dwarves looked up and his eyes brightened in recognition and he exclaimed, "Don't be so rude! That's Prince Lucas, second son of King Tristan!"

The young man blushed. "I'm afraid you're right!"

"Pardon my asking, but what are you doing all the way out here?" one of the dwarves asked.

Prince Lucas sighed dreamily. "Oh, I suppose part of me is looking for trouble. Part of me is looking to clear my head. Castle gossip and castle rules and castle etiquette get to be a bit much for me sometimes."

"'A bit much' is an understatement," one of the dwarves sobbed. "Castle life is ultimately what killed this beautiful creature." He gestured to the glass coffin and the prince approached it, gaping at the beauty lying within.

"Such a splendid, exotic work of art snatched from the world..." The prince mused.

Another dwarf nodded. "Even in death, she looks like she's sleeping."

"It's as if any minute now," said another, "she'll open her eyes and start singing another one of her sweet songs."

It was then, as if on cue, that Snow White's lids flickered. The prince's jaw dropped. Seeing his reaction, the dwarves inched closer to the glass coffin, and all witnessed the princess slowly opening her eyes.

*

Meanwhile, on the other side of the evergreen woodlands, Queen Brigid awoke once again with her confidence intact. She'd convinced the kingdom that Snow White had embarked on a long trip down South (little did they know, never to return), and now she was restored to her rightful place as the fairest in all the land. Thus, she asked with a knowing grin, "Mirror, mirror on the wall. Who's the fairest of them all?"

"You, my queen, are fair; it is true," said the mirror, "But Snow White, near the mountains, is still a thousand times fairer than you. I know you awoke feeling quite agog, but the dose you gave was only enough for a dog. Though an elaborate plan you did unfurl, the dose was not enough to end the girl."

Queen Brigid screamed and yanked at her hair. Within mere hours she'd found and paid an assassin a thousand and one pieces of gold for the head of Snow White.

*

Immediately, the dwarves pried open the casket. Snow White tried to sit up, but it seemed a great chore. One of the dwarves checked for a heartbeat on her dainty wrist and could barely detect a faint rhythm. And although her skin was still cold to the touch, a sheen of sweat coated her forehead. The dwarves gave her a glass of water, tiny bits of bread and cheese, and a few sips of milk and honey. While she ate, everyone filled in the prince on the circumstances.

"Who on Earth would want to harm a hair on your pretty head?" Prince Lucas reached out to touch Snow White's ethereal curls, but she recoiled.

"Well, I suspect," Snow White said weakly, "that that old woman who gave me a poisoned apple was my aunt's doing."

"You *must* let me help somehow," the prince said eagerly. "I have a horse and supplies. I could return you to your home in no time at all."

"No!" Snow White said. "I could never go back to that place, not while my aunt is still there."

The prince thought some more. "I could send you supplies periodically from my kingdom."

Snow White shook her head. "No, that would look strange and suspicious."

Prince Lucas thought much harder, tapping his chin with his finger. Then, he said cautiously, "I could perhaps take you back to my kingdom where you would be better protected and taken care of."

"Better taken care of!" huffed one of the dwarves.

"Well, the prince has a point," another dwarf said. "We can't protect her if we're out at the mines all day."

A third dwarf spoke up. "Well, I, for one, can't stand by and allow this situation to continue. I say we expose, and perhaps even *dispose* of, that rotten queen regent and install Snow White as proper ruler."

"I'm only eighteen," Snow White reminded him.

"Two years don't make much of a difference, and I think this is a special case," he offered.

8

Another dwarf looked toward the mountains. "A three-thousand-foot drop, and she'll never bother you again."

Snow White's hands shook and her poison-weakened heart sped. "Oh, I don't know. I don't know. So much could go wrong. I don't like this idea."

"Well, if and when you do decide to take back the throne," one of the dwarves said, "we will be with you every step of the way."

Snow White nodded, but she said nothing. Although she'd spent hours in a deep, deathlike sleep, she felt dreadfully exhausted. All she wanted was to go back to sleep.

"I have medicines in my supply pack," the prince offered. "It's castle-grade medicine, and if you like, I will stay the night and administer your doses and help take care of you until some of your strength has returned."

By this time, Snow White was quite wary of accepting consumables from strangers. "Whatever you give me, I want to see you taste it first. And whatever you give me, you give it to me in front of the dwarves."

The prince agreed, happy to help. And he and the dwarves cared for her as she rested for the remainder of the day and all through the night. Whenever she woke from an awful dream, one of them was there to comfort her. And whenever she twitched and moaned in her sleep, the prince would give her medicine to ease her symptoms.

Not long before the first light of day, a shadowy figure slipped in from the window. He'd nearly reached the sleeping Snow White when the prince, who'd been sleeping dutifully on a rug near her bed, discovered him, pulled his sword, and slashed at him, but the assassin was quick to dodge and pull a dagger of his own. Precise, expert jabs kept the prince at bay, but once Lucas found an opening, he lunged forth, impaling the stranger through the stomach. The assassin's cry woke everyone in the cottage. Dawn had barely lit the sky when Snow White was finally convinced that Queen Regent Brigid must be stopped. She, along with the dwarves and the prince, made haste for the castle.

*

"Mirror, mirror on the wall, who's the fairest of them all?"

"You, my queen, are fair; it is true," said the mirror, "But Snow White, near the mountains—"

Queen Brigid kicked the mirror so hard it cracked. How, *how*, could that assassin have failed? How hard could it be to kill a weak little girl? She worried all day and did not eat. Later, when she tried to sleep, slumber would not come. Instead, she paced her bedchamber, yanking at her hair and tearing away a few strands. Maybe if she had fallen second to Princess Ysobel, it wouldn't be so bad. Her hair fell in elegant waves of garnet against her milk-white throat. She probably would not have minded so much falling second to Queen Helga, whose cerulean eyes rivaled the sky on the clearest day. Instead, Queen Brigid ranked behind a girl with lips as red as blood, hair as white as snow, and skin as black as ebony.

A thump at her window startled her out of her frenzied thoughts, and she turned to see the silhouettes of men pouring into her room from outside. Then she glimpsed the silhouette of a woman, whose mass of curls framed her head like a halo. Before Brigid could react, she was grabbed and dragged away, screaming through the night, to meet her end at the foot of the mountains. The kingdom never heard from her again.

The dwarves had been right, indeed. An exception was made. Immediately after Snow White explained to the public why she had disappeared and the truth about Brigid, the young princess was crowned Queen.

Not a single townsperson was sad that cruel Brigid was gone, and the dwarves remained her closest friends and advisors throughout her reign.

Prince Lucas, celebrated as a hero in his kingdom as well as hers, often visited her to enjoy picnics, horse-riding, and walks around the garden.

And Queen Snow White lived happily ever after.

# The Sea and the Stars
## for Ed

There was no moon that night. Only the stars lit up the gleaming surface of the sea. A languid breeze tugged at tiny waves, and schools of fish floated sleepily along the seafloor. But elsewhere at the bottom of the sea, blinding festival lights surrounded the castle. The merpeople made their own moon and stars with strings of festival lights. Waves of deafening music pumped over a throng of young, frenzied mermaids and mermen. The dishes lay on the feast table half-devoured. Elders mingled along the sidelines, and the king and queen themselves oversaw the festivities.

This was how they celebrated the spring equinox. Moonray loved seeing everyone so lively, but she herself, timid wallflower that she was, smiled meekly from her seat at the feast table. She'd come as a third wheel with her friends Shell and Lily, who now clung to each other on the dance floor. She watched them wistfully. Moonray used to hope some dashing merman like Shell would ask her to dance, but she'd long since given up on that. She knew she was invisible and so lived somewhat vicariously through Shell and Lily.

Their story was like a fairy tale. Lily had met Shell while fishing close to the surface one night. She'd caught a sackful of gobies and was on her way home when she'd noticed a handsome young merman struggling to catch a swordfish. It'd slashed at him in defense and sped away. Lily had laughed and the handsome merman had heard her. *What's so funny?* Lily had told him it was impossible to catch one with his bare hands. However, Shell had recently joined a fencing club and needed a swordfish bill soon. Luckily for him, Lily was a champ at fencing. And swordfish wrestling.

Okay, so maybe it wasn't quite a fairy tale. But it was still sweet, and Moonray often daydreamed of meeting someone like that. Perhaps in her pottery class. *Oh, you like pots? Me too!* Or her aerobics class. *Oh, you like being fit? Me too!* But Moonray knew she couldn't talk to dashing mermen if someone paid her. What would be the point, when there were so many other gorgeous, charming, and interesting mergirls swimming through the kingdom? And she was a little sick of being the third wheel. Shell and Lily were great, but, increasingly, Moonray couldn't stand feeling alone while surrounded by people—girls with shinier fins and gradient hair, guys with pearly teeth and taut muscles.

When Lily sighed and said, "Moonray, you're not even *trying* to have a good time," a familiar ache rose in her chest. Moonray simply left the table and swam away. She swam until the music grew too faint to hear, until the collective laughter was muted, and there was only the ambiance of the sea.

Moonray didn't mind being alone as long as she was actually by herself. That festive throng had sucked the life out of her, but now she could close her eyes and recharge. She took a deep breath. There was no moon to admire that night, but she could still rise to the surface to bathe in the starlight. Moonray emerged slowly, careful to watch for humans. Countless stars glittered across the night sky. One of them appeared to fall.

A shooting star!

Moonray struggled to settle on just one wish. *I wish I weren't invisible. I wish I had gradient hair—I mean, I like that it's pink, but even two shades of pink would be nice. I wish I weren't so pasty—I want a tan like Lily's. I wish I were happy. I wish I could find my own Shell. I wish...!*

Then, the little mermaid noticed something strange about the shooting star. It was approaching. And it was approaching fast, plummeting toward the shore. Moonray ducked upon impact. Sand flew everywhere. When she peeked again above the surface, a massive crater had scarred the beach. She swam to shore, wondering what sort of strange rock had fallen from the sky. A rare crystal? A magic gem? She'd even be happy with a shiny space rock to wear around her neck.

As she neared the beach, the stench of burning grew acute. Smoldering zig-zags of fulgurite forged from the hot collision spiked up around the crater like a barricade. Moonray inched toward the shore and peered through a gap between two rods of fulgurite. Clouds of smoke filled the crater and disappeared into the sky. Eventually, it cleared enough for her to see the silhouette of a person sitting in the middle. To Moonray's horror, whoever it was had legs and feet. She ducked underneath the water to keep from being seen. But then she heard a harmonious voice.

"I know you're there."

Alarmed, Moonray decided to swim away, but the lilting voice stopped her.

"You don't have to be afraid."

Legged creatures were tricky, and Moonray had always been taught never to trust them. But somehow, this voice comforted her like nothing else could. She warily swam back to shore.

"How do I know I can trust you?" Moonray said.

"You fear the humans," said the voice in the smoke. "I understand. I've spent millions of years watching them self-destruct. In all my millennia of living, I've never witnessed such a counterproductive species."

Moonray blinked. "If you're not human, then what are you?"

"A star, of course."

"A star!"

The being stood and stretched in the thinning smoke, revealing the slender, curvy form of a woman. "Yes, a star," she replied, sounding amused. "And my name is Glimmer."

"Glimmer," the mermaid repeated. "What a gorgeous name!"

"Thank you." The star phased through the smoldering barrier and sat in the sand in front of the girl in the water. Her silver skin and sleek hair shone like platinum. "Do you have a name?"

The mermaid's mouth worked as she tried, for a brief moment, to remember what she was called. "Oh, of course. I'm Moonray."

Glimmer's smile broadened. "Can you come out of the water, Moonray?"

"No."

"Okay." Glimmer removed her glistening sandals. "Then I'll join you, if you don't mind?"

"Not at all." Moonray was mesmerized as the star lay next to her on the beach, wiggling her argent toes in the water. She'd never seen such glittering hair, gleaming eyes, shiny lips. Glimmer carried with her a tangible aura, the faint glow of which warmed the water around them.

"D-Did you hear my wish?" Moonray stammered.

Glimmer traced circles in the sand with her finger, looking quite pleased. "You made a wish on me?"

"You didn't hear it, then?"

"Wishing on falling stars is a phenomenon I've never been able to figure out, but I'm flattered."

"Oh," Moonray said, disappointed. "Well, do you think you'll be getting back to the sky anytime soon?"

Glimmer looked at her and shrugged. "Yes. But I'm all out of energy for the night. Something threw me off course, and whatever it was knocked the wind right out of me. So, for now, I'm out of commission." She looked at Moonray and grinned. "But at least I found a friend to pass the time with, for the time being."

The mermaid smiled back. "You already consider me your friend? Unbelievable." She cast her eyes down as she thought. All this time, she'd clung to Lily, whose infectious personality brightened the mood of anyone she spoke to, including Moonray. Lily could speak enough for the both of them, so Moonray often didn't even need to open her mouth.

Glimmer tilted her head. "Why so unbelievable? Because I'm a star?"

"Well, yes. I guess that's obvious," Moonray replied. "But it's not easy for me to make friends. Actually, it's downright impossible."

"Well, that can't be true now, because you have me to make friends with, don't you?" asked the star.

Moonray planted her elbows in the sand and rested her head in her hands. "But you'll be leaving soon, right? I've never seen stars out during the day."

"Rest assured." Glimmer looked thoughtful, a little dreamy. "You'll see me again."

Moonray was speechless. The slender, sexy mermen couldn't spare her a passing glance, but she'd managed to hold the attention of a beautiful star? None of it made sense to her.

"You have such lovely hair," Glimmer said suddenly, interrupting Moonray's thoughts. "May I feel it?"

The mermaid blinked, unsure of which astounded her more—being touched by a star or someone complimenting her hair. Glimmer regarded her with kind eyes, patiently awaiting Moonray's response. Words caught in the mermaid's throat, so she merely nodded.

Then, Moonray felt warm hands comb through her hair. Glimmer's slender fingers traced down the nape of her neck before returning to the top of her head. The star's hands were so soothing, Moonray's arms collapsed, and she laid her hands and head on the sand. What sort of space magic was this? Whatever it was, Moonray welcomed the mild tingles it radiated down her spine. She closed her eyes.

"This is my first time visiting Earth," the star continued. "I'd always watched from afar, and finally making it here didn't exactly happen the way I'd planned, but here I am. On the bright side, next time I come, I know where to land."

"You call me friend," Moonray said. "But you don't know anything about me."

"You trusted me when I told you you didn't have to be afraid. We can start from there."

Moonray sighed. "Some would call that stupidity."

"Some would, but I don't think you're stupid." The star's thumb stroked Moonray's cheek. "I couldn't help but notice, though, what sad eyes you have."

Moonray's heart thumped. "I'm not sad."

"It's not wise to lie in the presence of a star, dear."

Moonray's eyes flew open. "What?"

The star seemed to think a bit. Then she laughed lightly. "Poor choice of words, I suppose. But, what I meant is that we stars are quite perceptive."

"Oh." The mermaid closed her eyes again, surrendering to Glimmer's soothing touch. "Either way, you don't know anything about me. And I don't know anything about you."

Glimmer was silent for a while and continued combing through Moonray's tresses. Eventually, she said, "What beautiful hair. It's like nothing I've seen before on humans."

Moonray laughed.

"What? Have I said something funny?" The star seemed more amused than puzzled,

"Well," Moonray began sheepishly, "it's just that, if you think my hair is pretty, you obviously haven't seen any of the other mermaids. You obviously haven't seen Lily."

"Darling, I swear, merpeople and humans have more in common than you think."

Moonray lifted her head and recoiled. "I have nothing in common with those disgusting creatures!"

"I understand your sadness now." The star nodded slowly.

"What do you mean by that?"

Glimmer said nothing. She looked up at her fellow stars twinkling in the sky. Silence settled. Moonray took a deep breath and joined Glimmer in gazing at the night sky. Outer space seemed so incomprehensibly boundless. Of all the objects that could have knocked a star off its course, and of all the places for this star to land, Glimmer had landed here, at this precise point in time. Moonray's mind was struggling to digest it all.

While she was lost in thought, she felt Glimmer's hand move over hers. Their fingers clasped together. Moonray's face warmed.

"Stars are so distant from each other," Glimmer said at last. "Whenever another star near my spot in the sky dies, I get a little more lonesome."

"At least you don't have to feel lonesome in the middle of a group of people who don't understand your loneliness," Moonray added, hoping to be of some comfort.

Glimmer smiled warmly at that. Moonray matched her smile, and they spent the rest of the night talking about everything and nothing. What do stars do for fun, anyway? Is there music up there? Who are Shell and Lily? Glimmer lay on her side, facing the mermaid, and asked if Moonray felt as if her friends really valued her friendship, and Moonray, to her shame and dismay, discovered she wasn't sure anymore. She also lay on her side, resting her head on her arm in thought. What were friendships like among the stars? Toward the end of the conversation, Glimmer squeezed her hand.

"The sun will be up soon. I should find a place to sleep."

Moonray squeezed the star's hand back. "So soon?"

Somehow, the thought of losing this warm presence made Moonray feel more alone than ever. She shuffled closer and Glimmer embraced her.

"What are you?" Moonray asked.

"I told you. I'm a star."

"But what are you doing to me?" The mermaid clung closer, pressing against the star's soft body, reveling in her smooth, silver skin. She wanted to bring Glimmer home with her. "It feels like you're drawing me in."

"Does it feel dangerous?"

Moonray thought about it. "No." It felt warm and welcoming.

"What do you feel?"

Moonray's heart raced. Her face was so close to the star's that their noses almost touched. "Like I'm not alone, I guess."

"You're not." Glimmer caressed her cheek with a sparkling hand. Neither said a thing for several moments, each locked in the other's gaze. Then Glimmer leaned in, and Moonray closed her eyes.

When their lips met, Glimmer wrapped her arms around the small of Moonray's back, pulling the mermaid a little further into the kiss. Moonray's trembling mouth melted against the star's warm, cherubic lips. And when Glimmer broke away, she did so slowly, letting the kiss linger. Moonray was frozen. She didn't know whether to say something or lean in for another kiss. All she could do was stare stupidly at this stunning woman lying beside her.

Glimmer snickered and ran her fingers through Moonray's hair. "I'll be around again soon, I promise. You'll feel me near. And we'll talk more, and you can tell me anything. Everything."

"Are you sure?" Moonray's heart had never sped so fast. "Wait, are you sure you have to leave?"

The star smiled, patting Moonray on the head, and rose from the water. "If you want me to live to see you again, yes."

The mermaid watched forlornly as Glimmer sat up on the sand, stood, and sauntered past the scorched sand, toward the forest. Why did she have to leave now? Now that she'd had a taste of the star's lips, she wanted to plant her mouth on Glimmer's soft breasts, or on her soft, warm neck, or just above her taut navel. How *dare* she? How dare the sun rise *now*?

"Wait!"

Glimmer turned around. "Yes?"

Moonray looked sheepishly at her hands. "So, I'll see you again soon, right?"

The star smiled. "Every night."

"I'd like that," Moonray said diffidently. "And next time?"

Glimmer turned around again. "Yes?"

"This was nice, so next time, let's kind of finish it."

"I'd planned on it, and we will," Glimmer said. "I promise."

15

The star returned to plant a soft kiss on Moonray's forehead before turning to leave once again. Her gaze locked on Glimmer's sterling eyes for a brief time. Every night, she'd promised. Moonray was going to hold her to that. Glimmer touched her nose to Moonray's before turning to leave one last time, and the mermaid watched as the sun rose and the star disappeared into the shadows of the greenery.

# Rapunzel, the Night Maiden
## *for Mom*

Rapunzel sang. It wasn't a particularly glorious afternoon, but she felt like singing while braiding her hair. The sky wasn't clear, but the clouds were fluffy and bright, and Rapunzel often dreamed of flying up and sleeping on them. She sat close to the only window of her room at the very top of her tower, basking in the fragrant spring breeze blowing in through the open pane. Pansies, snowdrops, witch hazels, roses. Her mother had quite the green thumb, and the peace of the meadow was music to her ears, especially the birdsong. If she listened well, she could hear the faint rustling of the bushes in the nearby forest on a gusty day.

Then, she heard footsteps through the foliage.

Rapunzel's heart dropped a little. Her mother wasn't supposed to visit her for another three hours. Had something happened? Was there an emergency? Before she could peek outside, an unfamiliar voice called up to her.

"Hello? Is someone up there?"

"N-No?" Rapunzel stuttered. A person! Another person! A man, at that. She'd often read about them and sometimes saw them galloping by without even knowing there was a girl in the dilapidated tower. Perhaps because she'd happened to be singing at the right time, this man had noticed her.

"No?" he said. "But you just replied to me."

"Yes, then."

"So, there *is* someone up there." The man sounded amused.

"Oh. Gosh." Rapunzel's heart drummed. Now, the only other person she'd ever talked to besides her mother probably thought she was an idiot. "I'm so silly. I'm just so nervous. I'm really not supposed to talk to anyone, but here we are, and I got so excited."

"Excited?" he said. "And why aren't you supposed to talk to anyone?"

"My mother forbids it."

"But why?"

Rapunzel panicked. "I've already said too much. Good-bye."

She hastily shut her window and retreated further into her room. *That was careless of me*, she thought. Her mother had told her that the outside world was dangerous and that everyone out there would conspire to ruin her. Rapunzel didn't want to believe that, but, just in case, perhaps it would be best not to talk to anyone while her mother wasn't around. And from now on, maybe she would keep her singing to herself.

*

"Excuse me, miss? Are you still up there?"

There he was again, later that night. What was this strange man's problem? She thought she'd made it clear that she didn't want to speak to him. She decided not to answer him and hoped he would take the hint and go away forever.

He persisted. "Hello? Surely I wasn't dreaming earlier when I heard your lovely voice."

Rapunzel bit her lip. Maybe he wasn't so bad. "You really think my voice is lovely?"

"Like a songbird," he said. "I must see you."

"...I'm sorry, what?"

"Is there any way I could climb up and see you?"

"Uh, yes." Rapunzel cursed under her breath for telling him so. Only her mother was supposed to know about the secret way up the tower.

"Then, can I come up?"

"No," she blurted. "My mother would have a fit."

"Oh, right. How old are you?"

Rapunzel huffed. "None of your business. I'm old enough."

"So, a child."

"Excuse *you*, I'll have you know that I am three months and twenty years old, thank you very much."

"You're quite the shrew," he said. "But you're sure you don't need saving?"

"I'm positive?" Rapunzel raised her brow at such a strange question. "Why would you think I need saving?"

"For starters, you're stuck in a tower, aren't you?" he said.

"I'm *living* here." Rapunzel thought living in a tower was normal.

"Anyway," he continued. "The last damsel I tried to save was also trapped in a tower, under the spell of a dragon, who then sent me out to get him some tea. But by the time I returned, the dragon was gone, so I gave the tea to the damsel, who swiftly rejected my gift and accused me of trying to murder her."

"Oh dear."

"Also, there was another woman there whom I was sure was under the influence of the dragon. It's kind of a long story."

"Oh wow," Rapunzel said. "That sounds like quite the adventure. I do wish I could let you up."

"If you could, I'd tell you all about it," he said, playfully.

Rapunzel twirled a finger around the end of her braid. This person seemed friendly. Perhaps her mother was wrong. Surely some people in the world were harmless.

"Well, my mother usually returns around midnight..."

"Then we've got plenty of time! Why don't you throw down your rope?"

She chuckled. "Oh, I don't have a rope."

"Then, how else am I supposed to get up there?"

"Actually," she said. "My mother visits every day at noon, six, and midnight. I'd let down my hair, and she'd climb right up."

"...You're joking."

"I'm not," she said. Why was that so hard to believe? Her mother's twisted locks were almost as long. When not wrapped up, they fell down her back like tiny ropes of silver. "I could let my hair down right now if I wanted. I just finished braiding it."

"Well, then. Throw it down. Let's see." Again, the man sounded amused, and Rapunzel found that slightly annoying.

She wrapped her huge, raven braid a few times around the hook just outside her window and let the rest fall to the grass below. However, she wasn't patient enough to wait for him to climb up. She had to see him! The only humans she'd ever gotten a good look at (besides her mother) were illustrations in her many books. Rapunzel stuck her head out the window.

She stared down at him. He stared up at her.

"Oh."

Rapunzel frowned. "What? What's wrong?"

"Nothing."

"Then why did you say 'oh' like that?"

"I'm just—I'm just a little surprised," he said. "I didn't expect you to be—I mean, I've never seen someone who looks like you around here, is all."

Rapunzel narrowed her eyes. "What do you mean?"

The man cleared his throat. "Well, I've heard tales as a child about the Night Maidens, beautiful women as black as night with incredibly long hair. I suppose your braid makes sense now."

"Oh?" She was intrigued. None of her books had mentioned anything like this.

"I heard they were persecuted, and the survivors subsequently vanished," he continued. "So, I thought they'd all be gone. And yet, here you are." He seemed to be in awe.

"P-persecuted?" Suddenly, Rapunzel felt upset. She'd truly never heard about such a thing—not from her books, not from her mother, not even from eavesdropping on the rare conversations that occurred below. Either her mother was hiding something from her, or this man was lying. "Vanished? What are you talking about?"

The man seemed momentarily speechless. "You really don't know?"

Rapunzel shook her head. "I suppose I don't." Now, she really wanted to let him up so he could explain more. But again, he could have been making it all up. "How do I know I can trust you?"

"It was a rather big event." He spoke as if he pitied her. "Some called them the Idanko, the magical girls. That doesn't ring a bell to you? Most were kind healers, but it only took a malevolent few to spread fear."

She couldn't believe what she was hearing.

*A magical Night Maiden?* she thought. *Little old me? I could have powers?*

She couldn't comprehend it. "Never in a thousand years!"

"I swear by my mother's grave," he said solemnly.

Rapunzel raised a brow. "Well, if that's true, and I resemble these so-called magic women, then why aren't you afraid of me?"

"My grandmother was raised by an Idanko."

"I see." She looked around. Perhaps she could let him up, and in case he was a bad man, she could defend herself. Unfortunately, her mother wouldn't let her keep anything too sharp like a dagger, or blunt like a club. Rapunzel spotted her heaviest book and decided that if he tried anything funny, a good, firm hit to the noggin should knock him out. "All right. I'll let you up and you can tell me more. But first, what's your name?"

19

"Sir Richard Ludwig," he replied proudly. "And you?"

*What a long and elegant name,* she thought. "Rapunzel."

"Rapunzel what?"

She shrugged. "Just Rapunzel."

"Haven't you got a surname?"

Rapunzel rubbed her chin in thought. She'd never considered that before. "I guess I don't."

"Very well." Sir Richard tugged on the thick braid. "Are you sure I can climb this and it won't hurt you?"

"I'm positive."

The man climbed steadily until he reached the window. Rapunzel stepped aside to let him through.

"You've got a quaint room up here."

"Do I?" she said, unwrapping her braid from around the hook. "I decorate it with all my favorite things. If I read about something I like, I ask my mother to bring it up for me."

Rapunzel had draped her walls with red and gold silks from the East; precious hand-bound books from the South filled her bookshelves; an ornate rug from the West covered her floor; and elegant furniture from the North stood all around the room. Vases containing her favorite flowers sat on every table.

"You've acquired none of these things using magic?"

"I've never had magical powers in my life," she replied. "But tell me more about these Night Maidens, the Idanko."

"Surely your mother is one of them," he said. "She's never told you?"

Rapunzel shook her head.

Sir Richard took a seat on the rug and Rapunzel followed suit. "My grandmother was an orphan, you see. A Night Maiden found her abandoned in a basket and took her in. She taught my grandmother everything she knows about healing herbs and potions—just about the only thing she couldn't teach was the healing magic itself. My grandmother passed the information down to my mother, and then my mother became the kingdom's royal physician. After her death, my grandmother took the job, and they pay her handsomely. So you see, I've never had anything against the Night Maidens. My grandmother would tell me wonderful stories, and I'd always wanted to meet one. But by the time I was twelve years old, they were all gone." He gave her a small grin. "Or so I thought."

Rapunzel's heart sank. Her mother would go on and on about how dangerous the outside world was for her. Perhaps, this was why. "That makes sense, I suppose."

"Maybe your mother fled and settled in this tower where no one would find her," Sir Richard said.

Rapunzel didn't want to believe it. She didn't cry often, but now a warm film of new tears glossed her eyes. "Why wouldn't my mother tell me any of this?"

Sir Richard scratched his head. "Maybe she wanted to protect you and thought that this was the only way."

She couldn't fathom being a descendant from a lost magical race. All she'd ever known was her room and her books. Magic was a thing she read about in children's tales. She never thought it could be *real*. Rapunzel looked at her hands. *Am I capable of healing magic?* she wondered.

"I'm sorry to be the one to tell you," Sir Richard said.

Rapunzel looked at him. Then, she spawned an idea.

"You introduced yourself as Sir Richard, which means you're a knight, correct?" she said, blinking away the tears.

Sir Richard seemed taken aback by the sudden change of subject. "Yes, but…"

"So you must have a sword on you? A dagger perhaps?" A new sort of determination budded inside her now. If this experiment of hers worked, then she'd go from unremarkable little tower girl to Rapunzel the Night Maiden. She'd become a girl with a history. Maybe even a surname.

The knight fingered the dagger attached to his belt. "Why, of course, but it's probably not a good idea to play with it."

"I'm not going to play with it!" she said. "I have an idea. I want to see if I can heal. Maybe, I can summon my magic somehow."

"Goodness! You're not going to draw your own blood, are you?"

"How else am I to find out?"

Sir Richard touched her hand, and her face heated up. Somehow, that simple gesture made her heart race.

"Such impeccably smooth skin doesn't deserve blemishes, no matter how temporary." He pulled up his sleeve and offered his own arm. "I've been a knight long enough to have gathered a nick or two."

Rapunzel ran her fingertips along his forearm. His skin was the color of sand, and her own, the color of tea.

"Are you sure?" she said.

He handed her the dagger. "A little scratch never hurt anyone."

Rapunzel took the dagger into her trembling hands. It was heavier than she'd expected. "Are you completely sure?"

He chuckled. "You're definitely a Night Maiden. I have no doubts about that."

Rapunzel bit her lip and grazed Sir Richard's arm with the blade. A thin line of blood rose to the surface. *Blood*, she thought. *Real blood!* She dropped the dagger.

"What have I done?" Rapunzel cried. "I have no idea how to summon magic. I've made a mistake!"

Sir Richard laughed. "You gave me a paper cut is what you did. Now take deep breaths, and try to focus. Maybe something will come to you."

Rapunzel hovered her hand over his tiny wound. "Heal please!"

She waited. Nothing happened.

"Try something else," he offered.

"Please heal!"

"Well, something a little more different."

"Dear wound, I would like you to heal!"

A small drop of blood escaped the wound and ran down his arm.

"Think really hard, Rapunzel."

She closed her eyes and pictured his arm fully healed, holding it in her mind's eye for as long as she could while fending off stray thoughts. *Please close up.* The harder she thought, the more her hands tingled, and it scared her a little. Rapunzel gasped and opened her eyes.

"What? What's happened?"

"I think it was working," she said, sheepishly.

Sir Richard grinned. "Well then. Let's try again."

Rapunzel nodded, closed her eyes, and tried again. This time, after the tingly feeling, her palms grew warm. A surge of energy flowed from her mind and down her arms like waterfalls.

"By the stars..." Sir Richard whispered.

Rapunzel opened her eyes. "Did it work?"

"See for yourself." Sir Richard's eyes were wide.

When she looked down at his arm, the cut was gone. Rapunzel squealed from a mix of joy, shock, and fear.

"You did it!"

"I did it!"

Sir Richard took her hands into his. "You know what this means, don't you?"

"Yes! It means...!" She paused. Her smile faded a little. This meant that her mother had been hiding this secret from her. It also meant that her own people were persecuted and driven away, or *killed*; it was most likely dangerous for her to venture beyond the tower. This meant that she was a Night Maiden, an Idanko, and yet, she could never go out and use her powers to help people. "It means nothing."

"What?" Sir Richard looked confused.

"It means nothing," she repeated, drawing her hands away from his. "My mother only wants the best for me, and if she never told me about this, then perhaps I shouldn't have ever found out."

"Rapunzel..."

"Furthermore," she said, "what's the use? If it's so dangerous for me out there, what point is there in me having these powers? No one would trust me to use them, it seems."

Sir Richard grew quiet, just then. Rapunzel looked at her hands again and felt the tears welling back up. Perhaps it really was better that she didn't know. She watched Sir Richard pull out a handkerchief and wipe the remaining blood from his arm. If she had only obeyed her mother, if she had only refused to let him in, none of this would have happened. It was hard to believe it had all happened in one day. But now that she knew, she couldn't unlearn it, and at the same time, she couldn't quite bring herself to even want to unlearn it. If her massive collection of books had taught her anything, it was that knowledge is power. Surely there was something she could do with her newfound skill.

*I'm a Night Maiden*, she thought tearfully. *My history runs long... somewhere. I just need to find it.*

This, of course, meant leaving the tower. And her mother. This made her sob aloud.

"I'm so sorry, Rapunzel." Sir Richard stood. "I never should have come." He gazed out the window. "Guess I should stop investigating towers."

"No, I'm glad you came," she sniffled, also standing.

"Your weeping says otherwise."

Rapunzel wiped away her tears with the sleeve of her dress. "Some of the Night Maidens ran away, right? They escaped persecution?"

He looked back at her. "Yes."

"Well, they all must have gone somewhere. It's just a matter of *where*."

"That was a long time ago. Do you intend to find them?" he asked.

Rapunzel clenched her fists. "Of course! They're my people. And I didn't even know I had a people until today."

"What about your mother?"

"I'll talk to her." She took a deep breath. It wasn't going to be easy. If she uttered the word "outside," her mother would bombard her with lectures, and Rapunzel never got the last word. But Rapunzel supposed that that was because she'd never thought outside the box until now. "I can get the last word."

"What now?"

"I can get the last word!" Rapunzel's chin quivered. "When it comes to outside, my mother won't let me get a word in edgewise. But I can write her a note before I leave."

She glanced at the clock. Rapunzel had until midnight to come up with something to say.

Sir Richard asked, "When are you going to leave, then?"

"I'll talk to her at midnight," she replied, wringing her fingers. "After she leaves, I'll write the note, and then... And then... Well, I guess that's when I finally leave this tower."

The young knight knitted his brows in concern. "Are you sure you're ready to venture out into the world, all on your own?"

"Not at all." Rapunzel looked around her room. "But I can't stay up here forever, and I can't think of a better time to go than now."

Sir Richard glanced at his pocket watch. "Well, come midnight, you talk to your mother. I'll be waiting for you below, hiding somewhere in the forest."

"Waiting? For me?"

"I came here to help a damsel." Sir Richard grinned. "I guess I get to do that after all."

"You'd really help me?" she said.

He nodded. "Why not? It'll be an adventure with a beautiful, magical girl."

Rapunzel's heart sped and her face grew hot again. "R-Right. So, you'll be just outside?"

"Not far away at all."

"And you'll bring me back here when it's all over?"

Sir Richard nodded. "If that's what you wish."

"Good." Rapunzel hurried to the window and began wrapping her hair around the hook. "You go hide, then. And we'll go from there." She let her hair fall.

Before he climbed back down, Sir Richard gave her a firm, reassuring nod. Rapunzel thought she was going to have a heart attack.

*

Rapunzel chewed her fingernails to the nubs waiting for midnight. She jumped when she finally heard her mother's voice outside.

"Rapunzel, Rapunzel, let down your hair."

"Y-Yes, Mother." She skittered to the window and obediently threw down her braid. When her mother was halfway up the tower, Rapunzel thought she was going to faint from anxiety. Or vomit from anxiety. Or faint *and* vomit from anxiety. All she could hear was the pounding of her heart between her ears by the time her mother was climbing through the window.

"Hello, darling." Her mother dropped her giant sack on the floor. It looked heavy as always. "You'll never believe what I found."

Normally, hearing "you'll never believe what I found" was cause to jump for joy, but Rapunzel couldn't move or speak.

"Well?" Her mother said, rummaging through her bag. "You're quiet tonight. Are you sick?"

"N-No. My chest hurts a little, though." And she felt a little lightheaded.

"Oh, darling, then go lie down."

"I can't, Mother."

Her mother looked at her, giving her daughter her full attention. "What do you mean *you can't*? You're acting so strange, Rapunzel. It's scaring me a little."

Rapunzel took a deep breath. "I want to go outside!"

"Rapunzel..."

"Please! I found out what I really am, what we really are."

Her mother sighed and closed the sack. "What are you going on about? You know how I feel about outside, and if you keep asking, I'm going to start getting angry."

"But, mother, there was... there was this guy, and..."

Her mother grew ominously silent and crossed her arms. "In your books?"

"N-No. I met a real person."

"A guy?" Now, her mother's voice shook. "You don't mean the knight in the woods, with the brown hair?"

Rapunzel shrieked despite herself.

"Rapunzel! What have I told you about speaking to people, to anyone besides me? I didn't know you two spoke, or I'd have done worse," her mother exclaimed. "He only told me that he heard you singing. And I was about to talk to you about that. You ought to know better than to let others hear you sing. I told you one day, someone will hear you."

"He spoke to you?" That fool, Rapunzel thought. "W-What do you mean you would have done worse? What have you done to him?"

Her mother's eyes widened. She was incredulous. "You're so worried about someone you don't even know, about someone whom I'm certain is out to hurt you. He said he saw you, Rapunzel. Do you have any idea how dangerous that is? I had to blind him."

"You what!"

Rapunzel's mother raised her hand as a warning, and her daughter flinched. The next time, her mother wouldn't be so kind. "I guess I have no choice but to punish you. I'll have to start locking the window after I leave."

"No!" This ruined everything. Not only was her only friend and willing guide to the outside world blind, but now she couldn't even leave the tower.

"Yes." Her mother gathered her bag and slung it over her shoulder. "At least until you learn to obey me."

She watched helplessly as her mother approached the window. She needed to think of something, quickly.

"Rapunzel, let down your hair."

"Mother, before you leave, I have to tell you something."

"I don't want to hear it." Her mother opened the window pane. "I don't have the energy to argue with you. Let down your hair. I'll see you tomorrow afternoon."

"Mother…"

"I don't want to ask you a third time."

"I know that I'm a Night Maiden!"

She had never seen her mother whirl around so fast. "What did you say, child? Who told you about Night Maidens? That knight?"

"I know what I'm capable of, and I want to find others like us."

Her mother was so angry, her whole body trembled. "Where's that knight? I'll kill him!"

"No, wait!"

Rapunzel tried to pull her mother away from the window, but her mother flung her away. The pane flew open, and billows of wind thrashed through her mother's robes. Her silver hair fell from its heavy topknot and landed with an audible thump on the floor.

"They've found us!" she cried. "I should have known we couldn't hide forever."

"No, he's a good guy. He's going to help me!"

Her mother huffed. "That's what they want you to think."

Then, her mother did something Rapunzel had never seen before. She leaped out the window. Rapunzel screamed. But when she ran to see if her mother was okay, she saw her flying in the wind toward the forest. All this time, her mother could do this kind of magic? Rapunzel had so many questions. But there wasn't much time. Her initial plan was to knot her sheets together as a makeshift rope to climb down the tower, but that would take too long. Perhaps, Rapunzel could fly too. She looked out the window. It was a long way down. If she fell, there was no guarantee she'd be able to get back up. But she needed to leave. She needed to help Sir Richard.

She closed her eyes and, ignoring her racing heart, focused her energy on flying. *I'm light as the wind*, she thought. *Please, let me fly!*

Rapunzel stepped on the window ledge, looked down, and promptly returned inside. There was no way she could fly.

A man's scream rang out from the woods—undoubtedly, Sir Richard's.

Rapunzel ran to the window. It was now or never. She closed her eyes once again and leaped through.

And she dropped like a sandbag.

It was impossible to focus through the panic of free fall, but even a little magic helped her glide for several feet and softened the landing. She had no idea grass was so sharp or that the ground was so hard. It had always seemed soft. But enough of that. She ran through her mother's garden, across the meadow, and into the forest. Sir Richard screamed again, and she followed the noise. Soon, she heard him stumble around in the bushes, fleeing her mother's wrathful words, which echoed from somewhere nearby.

She found Sir Richard hiding in a small ditch and sprinted to him, thanking the stars that she'd found him before her mother had, although her mother's angry voice grew louder as she approached. When Sir Richard heard Rapunzel enter the ditch, he shuddered and screamed.

"No, no, Sir Richard, it's me. Rapunzel." She embraced him.

"Rapunzel!" He hugged her close. "I've been blinded."

"Yes, by my mother," she said. "I know she means well, but she thinks you're out to hurt me. I have to convince her otherwise. Are you hurt?"

Sir Richard shook his head. "Bruised, I'm sure. But it's nothing I can't handle."

"M-Maybe I could heal you," she said. "Maybe I could heal your eyes, too, after some practice."

Her mother's voice rang through the woods. "Rapunzel! I hear you! Are you with him?"

"Run," he whispered harshly.

"No, you're my friend and I'm not leaving you behind." She stood to face her mother and crossed her arms, echoing her mother's stance from before. "Yes, I am."

Soon, the women were face to face. Her mother settled her feet on the ground. "Go wait at the tower, child. I'll deal with you as soon as I'm finished with him."

"No."

"No?" The wind flared up around her mother, once again dancing through her robes. "Don't you see how this outsider has already influenced you?"

"This 'outsider' is my friend."

Her mother slapped her across the face. "You warped, misguided thing."

"You're the misguided one." Rapunzel touched her stinging cheek. "When I'm in that tower, I'm nobody. But out here, with experience, I could be someone great, someone worth remembering. Someone... Someone important enough to have a surname."

At that, her mother's face softened a little.

"I'm not going to learn about who I am from those books in the tower," Rapunzel continued.

Her mother rubbed her temples. "I tried to protect you from this."

"We do have a surname, don't we, mother?"

After a long sigh and a few beats of silence, her mother replied in a small voice, "Alade. Your actual name is Oriyomi Alade. But the tradition of our names has been erased and long forgotten."

"Someone somewhere must remember it," Rapunzel cried. "Someone other than us? We're more powerful than this. Aren't we Night Maidens? Why did we allow this to happen to us?"

Her mother shook her head. "Even if I refuse to tell you, you'll find a way to learn. I can't stop you now that you're out of the tower, can I?" Rapunzel heard her mother's voice crack, followed by stifled sobs. "You were all I had left, and I didn't want the world to take you away from me, too."

"I'm sorry, Mother. I should have been more sensitive." Rapunzel stepped forward and wrapped her arms around her mother, hugging her tightly. "Come with us. We could even find a place for us to live, somewhere far better than that tower."

Her mother held her close. "You know I wouldn't let you run out in this world without me. But, is there really nothing I can do to stop you from wanting to do this?"

"Not a thing. But we have our powers to guide and protect us, right? And we have Sir Richard, who's going to help us. And I'm sure I'll make more friends along the way," Rapunzel said.

Her mother gently pushed her away. "Well, if that's the case, your friend needs his eyesight back."

Sir Richard perked up at this.

"You mean it?" Rapunzel asked.

"It can't be helped." Her mother knelt next to the poor knight and took his chin in her hand. Her mouth pursed as if she'd just eaten something sour. Rapunzel could tell she didn't quite trust him yet. When she spoke to him, there was acid in her words. "Look this way, boy."

Rapunzel bent over to have a better look. "I want to learn how to do this."

Her mother snorted. "Healing the blind? That takes twenty years of experience, darling."

"Will you teach me along the way?"

"Yes. I'll teach you along the way."

*

The next morning, the knight was cured of his blindness, and Rapunzel was packed and ready to face the world. Her mother, with much dismay, had packed as well, but Rapunzel detected a slight glint in her eyes. As far as she knew, her mother had always walked the earth alone. This would be their first time exploring the outside world as mother and daughter. Sir Richard had even brought with him two horses and all sorts of world maps and books for Rapunzel to read. Before the three left on horseback (it was decided Rapunzel would be riding with her mother), her mother blessed them all with a protective spell to ward off illness and general bad luck—strong enough to keep you from tripping and falling into a ditch, but not enough to keep away a savvy gang of bandits. Rapunzel tried not to think about this last part.

As Rapunzel wrapped up her hair and tied a scarf to cover her nose and mouth, she savored the sun on her skin, the grass under her feet, and the vastness of the bright sky. The horse beside her swished its tail.

This was definitely going to be a once-in-a-lifetime adventure.

*

Rapunzel, Sir Richard, and her mother traveled in silence for the first hour of their trip. (Rapunzel had made several embarrassing attempts to mount the horse. Once, her foot got caught in the stirrup, and Sir Richard had to help her.) The former two knew their way out of the forest, but Rapunzel's eyes were glued to the map. Where were they going? What did life look like beyond the trees? What did life look like beyond the map? She found a red square on the map labeled "Henrich's Tavern," and she knew from her books that taverns had plenty of delicious drinks. How about they stop there? *Or, wait. Travelers get weary, don't they?* She'd learned this from reading, too. Another red square on the map was labeled "Golden Lamb's Inn." But *wait!* She found another square, "Town Theatre."

"Sir Richard!" she called. "Is there any way we can attend a play at the Town Theatre?"

"Oh, Rapunzel," her mother chided gently. "We can't enter the town, not where people can see us."

Rapunzel's face fell. "Oh…"

"Your mother's right. Even though your hair's wrapped up, you'd still look suspicious. In the first place, there's virtually no one in town with ebon skin," Sir Richard added. "Not anymore."

"So, what then?" Her eyes flickered between the two. "We just travel and hide in the shadows? I thought we were exploring the world! Mother, isn't that what you did? How else did you bring things to the tower?"

"With much-practiced caution." Her mother glanced at her over her shoulder.

Rapunzel frowned and looked back at the map. Then she looked up and took in the trees around her, the canopy of green leaves above interrupting the warm sunlight, the little clouds of dirt kicked up by the horses' hooves. Straddling the saddle wasn't the most comfortable position in the world, and it was beginning to hurt her inner thighs, but she didn't want to complain. When she looked back up, she noticed her mother staring at her. She looked pained.

"I know this isn't what you were expecting, Rapunzel, but we can't go gallivanting around town, not with the way we look."

Rapunzel glanced at her hands, considering their color—not for the first time, as the characters in her books had never looked like her or her mother—but she'd never thought about how people in real life might react to someone who looked like her. When she'd daydream about adventuring in the outside world, she'd always imagined the people she encountered would see her as no different than they saw themselves.

"Then, tell me," Rapunzel said in a small voice. "How do you get around without getting noticed or caught?"

Her mother tilted her head back slightly and sighed, as if recalling a memory. "When King Otto sent his men for the Idanko—when they came for *us*—learning stealth magic became a priority, though it's not innate to us."

"I remember my grandmother telling me something like that," Sir Richard said softly. "Bits and pieces of it, anyway. Mama Ayo called it *the art of hiding*."

"Mama Ayo?" Rapunzel said.

"The Idanko that raised my grandmother," he clarified.

Rapunzel's mother stared at Sir Richard. "Mama Ayo, you said?"

"Yes." He glanced back. "Why? Does that name sound familiar?"

"Did this Mama Ayo have a set of twin girls?"

Sir Richard shook his head. "No, but she did have one daughter, Taiye."

Rapunzel's mother stiffened at the news.

"Mother? Are you okay? Who's Mama Ayo? Who's Taiye?"

"One more thing." Her mother's voice was hoarse now. "What was Mama Ayo's last name, do you know?"

"I don't know, I'm sorry," Sir Richard said regretfully.

"Mother, who are they?" Rapunzel pressed.

Her mother sucked in a lungful of air and released it slowly. "Taiye was my mother's name, but Taiye is also a common Idanko name. It could be a coincidence." She paused. "But Taiye means 'the first to taste the world.' It is the name you give to the firstborn of a set of twins, and my mother had a twin that I never had the chance to meet. I never got to meet my grandmother, either, but the name Ayo resonates with me. It sounds so familiar, but that could be my faulty memory and overactive hope."

The trio fell silent then, and Rapunzel returned her gaze to the map, though she didn't really see it.

*

Rapunzel and company eventually reached the edge of the woods, and Sir Richard pointed to a small castle in the distance. "That's my family's estate. This is my fiefdom."

Other than the castle, five huts occupied the estate, and as they rode by, Rapunzel watched villagers plow the farmland. It was painfully underwhelming. When they reached the stables, the stench made her gag. But the castle itself was charming. It sat on green little hill, and the turquoise spires complemented its dark brick.

"We'll be safe here," he continued, dismounting his horse. "And you are free to practice your magic as you wish."

Rapunzel perked up at the news. "So then, Mother, you can teach me stealth magic and how to heal blindness, and we can explore the town?"

"No, exploring the town is too dangerous," her mother replied matter-of-factly as she slid off her horse.

Rapunzel remained frozen on the horse, partly because she was upset, but mostly because she knew if she attempted to dismount, she'd fall. Again.

"Too dangerous?" she protested. "Then what was the actual point of you letting me out of the tower if you won't actually let me *do* anything?"

Sir Richard looked like he wanted to interject, but her mother was faster. She whirled around to face her daughter with a quickness, which Rapunzel knew often preceded a slap. Even though she was elevated by her horse, Rapunzel still flinched, but her mother's hand did not move. Instead, her mother said, "I let you out of the tower so you can have a closer view of the outside world in the safest way possible. I'll teach you stealth magic by day, and when I feel you're ready, you may observe the town by evening at a distance. Even now, distanced as we are from the town, we are still in relative danger. The safest place for us to be, always, is *in the tower.*"

"Are there people who look like us who aren't Idanko?" Rapunzel replied. "When Sir Richard saw me, he didn't even consider I was a Night Maiden until he saw my hair. Maybe not everyone knows about what we are."

"In the first place, Sir Richard is a fool."

The knight frowned at this.

"Secondly, do you want to take the chance and run around the town? Do you want to chance being exiled *or killed*?" Her mother spoke through her teeth, outraged, but anxious tears welled up in her eyes. "That tower is where my mother kept me safe when *they* came for us." When she said "they," her gaze darted to Sir Richard and returned to Rapunzel.

By now, the poor knight had grown red in the face. He raised his hands disarmingly. "We could discuss this in my dining hall, perhaps. I'll have the cooks fix us supper while we talk. And Rapunzel, wouldn't you like to come down from the horse? I have to have my stableman tend to it..."

"No!" She hadn't meant that for the knight—she'd meant it for her mother. "I may as well still be in the tower."

"Rapunzel," her mother said, "get off the horse. Right now."

Rapunzel's grip on the reigns only tightened . "I'm going to town."

"No." Her mother's eyes narrowed. "You're not."

"I'll do you one better. I'm going to find the rest of my people."

"Oriyomi Alade, *get off the horse!*"

"Or what!" Rapunzel spat. "You'll blind me?"

Before her mother could reply, Rapunzel tucked her face back into the scarf, gave her horse a squeeze of her legs, and raced it out onto the farmland. Frightened and confused peasants screamed and leaped out of her way. The wind against her face was exhilarating. In all the excitement, Rapunzel opened her mouth wide and laughed long and hard.

And a bug flew straight to the back of her throat.

As she choked and gagged, Rapunzel lost control of the horse and slid off the saddle into a pile of wheat. She heard the upset horse gallop away, and the peasant family that'd grown the wheat cowered nearby. When she sat up, she saw they'd hid in their hut, but were peaking out at her from the doorway with a mix of terror and curiosity. Suddenly, their eyes widened. The wife screamed, and all the members of the family shut themselves in the hut. Wondering what they'd seen, Rapunzel looked behind her and saw her mother flying to her. *So much for being cautious.*

"Can you stand?" Her mother asked.

When Rapunzel tried, her various aches and pains spiked, and she winced.

Her mother sighed. "It's a good thing your mother's a healer. Here, I'll help you to the castle."

As she helped her up, Rapunzel glanced back at the hut. "What about them? They saw you fly. I thought we were supposed to be *careful!*"

Without warning, her mother stood, turned to the peasants, and threatened them to keep quiet about what they saw, or she'd blind them all. For good measure, she chanted something in a language Rapunzel didn't understand.

Then, she returned her attention to her daughter. "I needed to fly to be able to catch up with you."

"What did you do to them?" Rapunzel squealed.

"I snatched their voices from their throats," her mother replied nonchalantly. When her daughter gave her a horrified look, she bent down and whispered. "Temporarily. Anyway, farmers out here are superstitious to a fault, Rapunzel." She helped Rapunzel stand. "No one in town with half a brain would believe them."

\*

Rapunzel awoke in a lavish bed under a white canopy to a servant girl dabbing her forehead with a damp towel. This must have been one of Sir Richard's guest chambers. Rapunzel could tell the servant girl tried her best to look unperturbed, but apprehension danced around the girl's eyes. Her mouth was a tight, thin line, and the hand dabbing Rapunzel's forehead trembled a little. When she was done, she back away, bowed, and hurried out of the room.

Rapunzel understood by now that she looked a little different, but why did that servant girl seem so afraid? What was there to be scared of? Somehow, Rapunzel's feelings were hurt. But then, of course, she remembered that she *did* run a galloping horse into a peasant's yard and crash into their hard-earned wheat, before being rescued by her mother, a flying woman. Anyone who might have seen that would have been at least a little spooked. Fine. But thinking about her embarrassing antics didn't exactly make her feel much better. When she moved, though, she noticed a distinct lack of pain. Not so much as a dull ache plagued her body.

A soft knock at the chamber door interrupted her thoughts. Rapunzel cleared her throat and bid her visitor enter. Sir Richard opened the door a crack and peeked through with a sheepish smile.

"Your mother's a feisty one," he said.

"Oh, my goodness. She said some sort of mean thing to you at the stables, didn't she?" Rapunzel tried to remember.

Sir Richard shrugged and closed the door behind him. "Well, it was more of an insinuation. It was the way she looked at me when she talked about the persecutions of the Idanko. I can't say I blame her, though."

"Oh." Rapunzel noticed he carried a book and her heart fluttered. "But what's that? Is that for me?"

"In a way." He smiled brightly and pulled a chair up to her bedside.

"Well, what kind of book is it? What's it about?"

Sir Richard held the book in both hands as if it were made of solid gold. "It's Mama Ayo's diary."

Rapunzel's jaw slackened at this, and she was speechless. Sir Richard continued, "It wasn't really something I thought to look into until after I met you. And then, you mentioned finding your people, and I thought that maybe I could help you. There could be some clues in here."

"You really think so?" Rapunzel said in a small voice.

"I don't want to get our hopes up too high," he said. "But I think there's a chance. I don't know yet. I haven't looked in it."

Sir Richard's gaze rose from the book to meet Rapunzel's. He continued, "I think it'd be only right if you looked inside it first."

"I would love to…" Rapunzel's voice trailed off as she took the diary into her own trembling hands. Bound in red leather with a gilded floral pattern, it felt heavy. Its edges were worn, and some of the flowers had lost their gold color. This could possibly be the most important book she'd ever read. But one thing stopped her from opening it. "Wait. I want my mother to be in here, too. Where is she?"

"In her guest rooms, writing up stealth magic lessons for you, actually."

"Well, go get her!"

Sir Richard paled. "Right, of course. We should have her here, too."

He hesitated before standing, and Rapunzel smirked.

"You're scared of my mother."

Sir Richard looked at her as if she'd just told him, with profound sincerity, that she'd just realized the sky was blue. "*Of course* I'm afraid of her!"

*

Sir Richard had sent a serving girl to fetch Rapunzel's mother, who, annoyed at having to leave her work, nonetheless attended. Now that all three were present in the room, Rapunzel opened the book to the first page.

She couldn't read a single word of it.

"What? What's this?" She tried to think of some of the language-learning books her mother had brought back from her travels. There weren't many, but Rapunzel had managed to read a couple. None of those languages looked anything like this. "I've never seen this language in my life."

Sir Richard craned his neck to look at the pages. "Well, this is disappointing."

During the horse ride, Rapunzel had skimmed one of the books Sir Richard had lent her. Her eyes had lit up at the mention of Night Maidens in an old reference book, but that section had mostly detailed Idanko life before the persecutions. The land from which they'd originated was vaguely named the "Old Country".

Rapunzel's mother looked at the book and brought her finger to her lips in thought. "My mother taught me some of our native tongue, but it's been so long. Most of what I remember now are spells."

"But you can read some of this?" Rapunzel looked up at her mother hopefully.

Her mother grimaced and gingerly took the book from Rapunzel's hands. "I can try."

"Your mother never taught you about where we came from?"

"Oh, darling." Her mother's forehead creased as she studied the pages. "We've been in this country for quite some time. By the time I came along, we were already starting to forget our roots in the motherland."

"But why would anyone forget?" The way the question came out was a little more demanding than Rapunzel had intended.

When no one replied, she continued, "Well, we were, at some point, going to try to find some exiled Idanko who might be scattered around, weren't we? Maybe they're hiding away in a cottage or another tower in some obscure field some miles from here. Maybe there's a small community somewhere. Maybe we can find someone with more answers!"

Her mother exhaled audibly through her nose and closed the diary. "I might know someone. I take supplies to her when I can, to give her son a break. But she's ninety-seven years old."

"She's the perfect source, then!" Rapunzel gushed.

"I really don't want to trouble her." Her mother frowned.

Sir Richard chimed in softly, "It might be worth the trip. Where is she?"

When her mother didn't reply right away, Rapunzel thought maybe she needed a little nudge. "You wouldn't have brought her up if you thought she'd be of no help."

The pinched look on her mother's face, however, told Rapunzel that that wasn't the reason she was hesitating to say.

"Not everyone needs to know her whereabouts."

"What?" Rapunzel said. Then it clicked in her mind: Her mother didn't want Sir Richard to know where this woman lived. "You think he'd hurt her somehow? You distrust him that much?"

Sir Richard rested an arm on Rapunzel's shoulder and squeezed. "I admit, I haven't done much to be considered trustworthy."

"Kidnapping my daughter isn't exactly high on the list of things I approve of."

"But I'll prove to you that I *am* your ally," Sir Richard said. "Mama Ayo may as well have been my own great-grandmother."

Rapunzel's mother laughed mirthlessly and her eyes narrowed. Rapunzel knew Sir Richard was in danger and leaped out of bed to stand between them. "Well, let's go visit this woman you spoke of! What was her name, Mother? You never mentioned her name."

But her mother wasn't looking at her. She was looking past her, unblinkingly, at Sir Richard. "She wasn't your great-grandmother, boy. She was like so many Night Maidens of her generation—forced to neglect their own to suckle brats like you, paid to be stand-in mothers by wealthy women who couldn't be bothered to raise their own children. *My own* mother watched as *her* mother coddled and nurtured a baby she did not birth, all so she could earn enough money to support her family. Barely."

Sir Richard clenched his jaw but said nothing. Rapunzel's eyes danced between the two of them as they stared at each other.

"Well," she said calmly. "Like I said, Sir Richard is my friend, and he's coming along, whether you like it or not. You won't even give him a chance!"

"I've had my fill of chance-giving."

Richard took a deep breath. "I'll prove I'm your ally, and if I ever betray you, I implore you to blind me and cut out my tongue.

"Sir Richard!" Rapunzel exclaimed.

Her mother's gaze never left his, and her lip curled into a sly smile. "I like your style, Richard. But I've got an even better idea."

*

Deaf and blind (temporarily), Sir Richard let Rapunzel guide him as they walked. They'd traveled for a couple hours on horseback to arrive at a dilapidated hut in the middle of nowhere. It sat in a brown field, next to a sickly, leafless tree. Rapunzel's mother led the way to the misshapen door and knocked.

"Mama Eniiyi? It's Ifeya. I've brought my daughter this time. May we come in?"

Rapunzel's brows jumped. "Ifeya? That's your real name? Mother, that's beautiful!"

"Thank you, dear." Feet shuffled behind the door, and her mother added quickly. "But hide the boy."

Rapunzel whispered, "I'm sorry," even though she knew he couldn't hear her, and set him in some bushes. She'd expected some sort of protest, but he seemed resigned to his fate at this point.

The door opened.

"Beautiful Ifeya!" A tiny, half-starved woman had appeared in the doorway and embraced Rapunzel's mother in a long hug. "You said you brought your daughter? From the *tower*? Tell me you're joking."

"Ah, trust me, I don't like it, Mama Eniiyi, but here she is. My little Oriyomi, out in the real world." Her mother stepped aside so that the old woman could see her.

Rapunzel bowed awkwardly. "Uh, hello."

"You really are the spitting image of your mother. Look at you!" She smiled so broadly, the corners of her eyes grew longer, deeper crinkles. "I've been telling Ifeya for years she couldn't keep you all cooped up in that tower forever. I see you must have been better at persuading her than I ever was."

Mama Eniyii's silver-white braids grazed the floor as she retreated into her home and beckoned the two to enter. "Come, come. My son managed to scavenge some honey some weeks ago. I'd like to treat you two to some tea."

"Oh, no, Mama Eniiyi," Ifeya protested as they followed the older woman into her one-room hut. "We couldn't possibly accept such a delicacy from you. Your son must have gone to a lot of trouble for that."

The old woman waved dismissively. "It'd be rude of you to refuse. Sit."

Rapunzel and her mother found two dusty stools at the makeshift table in the center of the hut. When Rapunzel sat on hers, it wobbled.

"Now then." Mama Eniiyi set crude clay cups in front of her guests. "Why is there a gentleman sitting in my bushes?"

Ifeya grimaced and Rapunzel stared at her, wondering what sort of excuse her mother would come up with. But Mama Eniiyi only laughed.

"Ifeya, dear, you have so much more to learn, and I have so little time left to teach you." She lit a fire under the pot to boil water. "There's far more to magic than healing and flying. I trust you haven't blinded him."

"She did." Rapunzel grinned.

"I thought as much, to be perfectly honest."

Rapunzel's mother's countenance resembled a child getting caught doing something she wasn't supposed to do.

"Oh, Ifeya, dear, your overprotectiveness is endearing." Mama Eniiyi looked up from the pot. "But you can't try to keep everyone safe forever."

Rapunzel's mother looked down at her hands. "I know, Mama Eniiyi. That's something I'm still trying to learn."

"And what about you?" Mama Eniiyi's eyes shifted to Rapunzel. "Why have you brought everyone here? I assume it was you who led your mother and that poor, confused gentleman here?"

"I want to go to the Old Country." The words tumbled out of Rapunzel's mouth before she could stop them.

"Mm…" Mama Eniiyi nodded. She didn't seem at all surprised.

"We were wondering if you knew anything about how to get back there," Rapunzel continued. "And also, we brought this diary written in the old language that we can't read. Can you, maybe, read it?"

Mama Eniiyi chuckled. "I can, but my old eyes aren't what they used to be." She paused in thought. "What a big journey for your first time out of the tower. This is your first time out of the tower, right?"

"Yes, Mama Eniiyi."

"How ambitious." She smiled. "Hand me the diary, would you, dear? Let's see what I can do."

Rapunzel obeyed, and she and her mother watched as the old woman scanned the pages. She read silently for a while, and Rapunzel, growing anxious, wrung her hands.

"You mentioned a son earlier," she said.

"Mhmm." The old woman nodded without taking her eyes from the book.

More silence befell them. Then Rapunzel tried again. "Is he also an Idanko? Can men be Idanko, too?"

Her mother snickered at this. Mama Eniiyi merely smiled and said, "Oh, no. Men wouldn't know what to do with magic if they had it. But trust me, Tola is the most competent non-magical healer for miles around."

"Tola." Rapunzel let the name rest on her tongue. "Is that your son's name?"

Mama Eniiyi nodded. "It is."

Before anyone could say anything more, Mama Eniiyi noticed the water was boiling, closed the diary, and prepared their tea with honey.

"Where is he now?" Rapunzel asked, bringing the floral-smelling tea to her lips.

"Gathering," Mama Eniiyi replied, "as always."

Then, she stood at the makeshift table with the diary still in hand, watching Rapunzel's mother drink her tea. After a while, she spoke.

"I expect you don't remember much about your grandmother, Ifeya."

"Unfortunately, I don't, Mama Eniiyi."

The old woman continued to watch her intently. Rapunzel began to wonder what this was all about.

"I said Tola is the most competent non-magical healer for miles around," Mama Eniiyi said. "And that's only because that gentleman, the one in the bushes, his grandmother is no longer with us."

Rapunzel set down her cup. "You knew Sir Richard's grandmother?"

"I'll do you one better. I knew the woman who raised her." Mama Eniiyi set the diary on the table and slid it to Rapunzel. "Ayokunumi was such a wonderful spirit." She gave Rapunzel's mother a pointed look. "So much so that the gods blessed her with twins."

Ifeya sat still as stone.

Mama Eniiyi opened the diary on the table to a page in which a couple envelopes had been tucked. "One twin stayed here. The other twin went adventuring south and never returned. These"—she tapped the envelopes—"were letters from the twin that left."

Rapunzel's head swam.

"My hands don't write too well these days," Mama Eniiyi admitted. "But if you're willing to wait until Tola comes home, I can have him translate everything you need from this diary to venture into the Old Country. It'll take no time to for him to copy the letters and a couple passages."

Ifeya stood. "Really?"

Mama Eniiyi rubbed her chin. "I guess I should have been more specific. He'll translate everything *Oriyomi* will need to travel."

It hurt Rapunzel's heart to see her mother's face fall.

"Mama Eniiyi? What? What do you mean?" her mother asked, with a hint of desperation in her voice.

"This is Oriyomi's journey," Mama Eniiyi replied. "I understand your feelings as a mother, and that's why I know you've been holding her back. You can't hold her back this time, Ifeya."

Rapunzel chimed in. "But what if she wants to see the motherland, too, Mama Eniiyi?"

"I was getting to that." The old woman grinned. "I'd send you along a little later, Ifeya. But you need to let this little one go on ahead."

Rapunzel remembered her embarrassing mishap with the horse and the peasant family and gave the old woman a sheepish grin. "In my mother's defense, I probably do need a little guidance."

"You have that gentleman out there, don't you?"

"Oh, Mama Eniiyi, you *can't* be serious!" Rapunzel's mother protested.

The old woman gave Rapunzel's mother a sharp, reproachful look, and Rapunzel's mother went quiet.

"Speaking of that poor gentleman outside," Mama Eniiyi said. "Let him in, already."

*

Mama Eniiyi could cast as many powerful protection spells on Rapunzel as she liked, but it would never ease her mother's mind, not entirely. So many layers of magic had been cast over her that the air around the girl glowed blue. Sir Richard, cured by Mama Eniiyi, sat on the dirt floor in the corner, blinking and adjusting to being able to see. Again.

Knowing that she could not change Mama Eniiyi's mind (and knowing that Mama Eniiyi had ways of manifesting her will), Ifeya gave her daughter nonstop advice about simple, useful magics that would help her along the way ("Especially remember to use chamomile to strengthen your healing magic, if necessary. I already told you the chant for that, didn't I?" "Yes, Mother."). This continued even after Tola returned home at sundown with his bag of found things: five pieces of linen paper, three clay bowls, bags of various herbs, smaller bags of spices, half a loaf of bread, and a little sack of assorted vegetables that looked like they'd nearly rotted beyond edibility. Being a non-magical being, Rapunzel thought, must have made scavenging twice as hard for him. She had so many questions, but her mother would not let up from her endless advising longer than enough time for a short introduction. Though he approached eighty, he still had remnants of muscle underneath his dark, wrinkled skin. What sort of adventures had this man gotten into in his years of living? As she watched him translate Mama Ayo's diary by candlelight at the makeshift table, Rapunzel hoped he'd write a book about his life one day, or at least kept a diary of his own.

"Rapunzel, are you listening?" her mother snapped.

"Yes."

"What did I just say?"

"Stay in the shadows and move at night because my stealth magic isn't strong enough to use in broad daylight," Rapunzel droned.

Her mother's jaw trembled. "*Must* I stay behind while she goes ahead, Mama Eniiyi?"

The old woman said nothing, as she'd already given her answer.

"If I may cut in," Tola said, without looking up from his translating, "there isn't much for us to have faith in, these days. If my mother has put her full faith in this young woman, then I trust it. She's practically clairvoyant."

Mama Eniiyi made a dismissive gesture, as she gathered the clay cups and placed them on the ground next to her buckets of collected water. "I've just got strong intuition. No one can see the future."

"I'm still not so sure I can do this," Rapunzel said.

Mama Eniiyi gave her a kind smile. "Do you think I'm wrong, dear? Or that I don't know what I'm talking about?"

"Well, no, but..." Rapunzel glanced down at her hands. Her skin seemed to be absorbing the protective magic, and she felt almost invulnerable. She turned her gaze to Sir Richard, sitting in the corner and very much resembling a confused and startled rabbit. He sat still as stone, as if afraid to move in case her mother might curse him again. Even after Mama Eniiyi had offered him tea with honey and a meager slice of bread, he had not budged from his spot on the ground.

"Sir Richard?" Rapunzel said.

He looked at her. It seemed to take some effort for his eyes to focus on her face.

"Is this something you'd like to do with me?"

Sir Richard's eyes traveled around the room before he answered. "Well, I believe I'm the one who's started this whole misadventure. It'd be unknightly of me to bow out of it." He returned his gaze to Rapunzel. "Especially after all you've done to defend me. I... I think I can make this trip with you, but even I haven't traveled so far south. It'll be difficult for the both of us. But I think I can do it if..."

Sir Richard's eyes slid to Ifeya, and Rapunzel immediately understood he meant *as long as this woman doesn't tag along.*

"If," he continued, looking at the ground, "I can send word to the Order that I'll be away for some time on a personal mission trip. There should be no problems there."

"Then it sounds like a plan," Mama Eniiyi said, with finality.

Rapunzel's mother looked at the old woman, then her daughter, then the knight, and brought one hand to her mouth and the other to her chest. Tola did not look up from his work.

Mama Eniiyi nodded and smiled. "A plan it is."

*

As early as Rapunzel and Sir Richard awoke the next day, Tola had already left for the day's scavenging and had left neatly translated papers for them on the table. Everyone had slept on the hard, dirt floor the night before, and Rapunzel's body ached. She stretched her arms over her head and rose to the tips of her toes, then she shook out her legs. One uncomfortable night of sleeping wasn't going to stop her from the biggest moment of her life. Behind her, Sir Richard yawned, gave her a sleepy smile, and left the hut to feed the horses.

When he was gone, Rapunzel looked at her mother sleeping against the wall near the water buckets. She bent and kissed her mother's temple. She thought about leaving a farewell and thank you note to Mama Eniiyi, but paper seemed hard to come by, and she didn't want to dip into Mana Eniiyi's precious supply. Instead, Rapunzel settled on whispering a "thank you" before taking the translations and leaving the hut.

Outside, gray clouds blocked the sun and most of the sky. Sir Richard petted one of the horses on its nose, and as Rapunzel approached, he let out a long sigh.

"We'll take one horse and leave the other for your mother. Can't have her flying everywhere."

Rapunzel nodded. "Are you ready, then?"

"Truth be told," he said, "every sensible bone in my body is telling me to run far, far away. I don't know anything about magic, and even though it's just you and me on this trip, I have no idea what I'm getting myself into, and I'm terrified."

Rapunzel grinned, despite her own fear. "A knight? Terrified? Then how should little old me feel?"

"Just as terrified. But even if I rode all the way home and tried to forget all of this, I don't think my conscience would let me sleep at night, especially if it meant abandoning you," Sir Richard replied.

Rapunzel blushed. "Oh, Sir Richard, you really don't have to—"

"You can just call me Richard, you know."

"I mean, especially after everything my mom has said and *done* to you, I wouldn't blame you at all for leaving," Rapunzel said, glancing at the bushes she'd sat him in the day before.

"Well." Sir Richard grabbed an apple from one of the sacks hanging from the saddle and bit into it. "Your mother isn't coming, is she?"

"No, I'm not."

Rapunzel and Sir Richard, startled, stared at the doorway of the hut where Rapunzel's mother stood, with tightened fists and a clenched jaw. She looked like she was fighting back tears.

"Mother? I thought you were asleep!"

"You were going to leave without saying goodbye?"

Rapunzel picked at her nails sheepishly. "I thought it might be easier and less painful that way, and I wouldn't have to wake you up."

"Well, come here, child. I... I can't leave the hut," her mother said.

"What?"

Her mother sighed. "Mama Eniiyi has bound me here, for a time."

Rapunzel stepped up to the hut door and squeezed her mother in a loving embrace. Her mother planted a kiss on her forehead, accompanied by drops of warm tears.

"I'll be safe."

"I feel like I've taught you nothing, but try to remember as much as you can."

"I will." Rapunzel's own eyes grew hot with the promise of tears, and she broke away from the hug before they could well up. Now was not the time to cry. "I'll see you soon. I promise."

*

Three days passed, though it only took Rapunzel half a day to realize she wasn't built for this sort of travel. She rode the horse, mostly reading, while Sir Richard followed along on foot and navigated. Sometimes, he grew so weary that she would suggest they switch places, but he vehemently refused to make a lady walk so that he could ride on a horse. When it rained, he gave her his cloak, and when it came time to sleep, he spent most of the night on look-out duty. Rapunzel wasn't entirely sure why he thought he could travel so hard on such little sleep, but when he inevitably slipped into deep slumber and she awoke long before he did, she would cradle his head in her lap so that it wouldn't have to rest on the cold, hard ground. The first two times she did this, he awoke flustered and quickly excused himself to gather firewood or collect edible plants for the day's travel.

The notes that Tola had translated mentioned the name of her great-aunt, the sister of her grandmother Taiye — it was "Kehinde". If Mama Eniiyi had lived to see ninety-seven, Rapunzel wondered if Kehinde was maybe still alive? Did she have any other relatives in the Old Country? She imagined Kehinde may have married and had children of her own. The letters stopped when she was still quite young, so Mama Ayo may have never known she had grandchildren living in the Old Country. Cousins? Rapunzel gushed at the idea of having cousins.

"That does sound exciting," Sir Richard replied, as they trekked through the woods. "But how would you be able to communicate with them?"

"I'd find a way."

Sir Richard chuckled sleepily. "How? By pointing and grunting? By pointing to yourself and saying, 'Me, Oriyomi'?" He laughed harder. Rapunzel laughed, too, and realized this was the first time she'd heard him laugh in days.

*

Some days, when they had settled down to camp, Rapunzel would notice Sir Richard staring into the distance at nothing. On their eighth day of travel, Rapunzel decided to take an entire day of rest. She proposed she handle the food, the fire, and look-out duty. When Sir Richard tried to object, she cast a gentle sleep spell on him that she'd worked on in secret (it was pretty easy to do, as she'd practiced on herself, every night). Her magic was still relatively weak at this point, and the sleep spell would only last for three hours, but this was enough for her to get a few things done. Unfortunately, she didn't know a spell that would erase her own growing fatigue. Occasionally, they would follow a path for some miles and inevitably cross another traveler, usually a merchant, coming from the opposite direction. Rapunzel would have to muster all the energy in her tired bones to chant a quick stealth spell. It made her features unrecognizable and unremarked for a span of six minutes. Anyone who'd seen her in this state would have forgotten her immediately, but because six minutes was hardly any time at all, Sir Richard handled all the talking any time they'd needed to buy something from a traveling merchant. Rapunzel, meanwhile, would spend most of that time hiding behind the horse.

*

By their eleventh day of travel, Rapunzel and Sir Richard had found themselves famished and drained by the sun. When she learned that Tola's translations called for a month-long ship ride southward, Rapunzel wept from exhaustion.

"There's no way," she said. "I can't even keep up stealth magic for ten minutes. How are we going to do this boat ride, Richard?"

The knight consulted a map he'd bought from one of the passing merchants. The Old Country wasn't listed, as it didn't appear on any map, but Tola's notes had hinted that it was located ten miles west of Yorgeria. Presently, they stood on the southern coast of Deutschnia, huddling in the shadow of an inn and a few trees with their horse. Whenever anyone walked by, Rapunzel used the hood on Sir Richard's cloak (which she now wore constantly) to hide her face.

"The boat ride will take a month," he said. "But if we try to walk around, it'll take three times as long."

Rapunzel looked at him. His cheeks had grown hollow, and deep, dark bags plagued his eyes. She reached over and brushed some grass from his unkempt hair and was immediately envious. She wanted few things more than to be able to let her hair out of its wrap. It was heavy, and she wanted her scalp to breathe.

"So what are we going to do, then?" she asked.

Sir Richard sighed and folded up the map. "We're going to get on this ship, and if anyone asks any questions or looks at you funny, we kill them."

"We what!"

A weak smile spread across Sir Richard's lips. "I'm kidding." He cleared his throat and coughed before continuing. "But honestly, what *can* we do at this point? Turn around and head back home? Put a mask on your face and pretend as if that wouldn't be at all conspicuous?"

Rapunzel stared at him. "Where can we buy a mask?"

"I'm sorry, what?"

Rapunzel shrugged. "It might work. What do we have to lose at this point?"

"I really don't think"—Sir Richard coughed some more—"I really don't think that's a good idea. My purse is rapidly shrinking. This ship ride will take nearly everything I have left."

"Then we'll make one," Rapunzel said simply.

"With what?"

Rapunzel grinned and pointed to a small vegetable shop across the road, next to the docks. "You see those sacks of potatoes? A few rips with your dagger should make a functional mask, although not one that's very nice to look at. And I can use some thread from my dress for the string."

Sir Richard looked at her as if she'd just suggested they eat his arm for breakfast.

"You really think they'll let you on the ship like that?"

Rapunzel nodded. And they stared at each other until Sir Richard shook his head and, with much effort and groaning, got to his feet. "I'll be right back, then."

Before he turned to leave, Rapunzel grabbed one of his hands with both of hers and squeezed. "Thank you, Richard."

"You're welcome, I suppose."

As she watched him cross the road, she wondered how on earth she could possibly thank him for being her one friend and guide on this journey, for being the man who got her to leave the tower, for being the knight that stuck to his word. Her heart ached. For all the books she'd read detailing fierce romances and deep friendships, she couldn't find the words to express her gratitude to this man who could so easily have left her and her cause and continued to live his life as a knight, eating well on his estate (and joining in occasional crusades, which Rapunzel figured were about as uncomfortable as their current journey; though, to her knowledge, Sir Richard was still too young to have participated in a full crusade).

A moment later, he returned with her potato sack mask and handed it to her. "Here you go, then."

"Have you gone on a crusade yet, Richard?"

"Pardon?"

Rapunzel took the mask and yanked some thread from her travel-worn dress. "Have you been on a crusade yet? It was just something I was wondering about."

"I came in on the tail-end of one some years ago. I was one of the last to be deployed... Why do you ask?"

When Rapunzel struggled to tie the mask around her head, Sir Richard crouched to help her. She continued. "Well, it was just something I was thinking about. I just feel like it's something I ought to know about you, since you're likely the best friend I'm ever going to have. Anyway, how do I look?"

"Oh. Oh, my." Sir Richard stifled chuckles behind his hand. "You look like the stuff of nightmares."

"Nightmare Maiden!"

They both laughed as they stood and gathered their things. Rapunzel made sure the hood covered her face well enough. One of the dock workers announced the last call to board, and the two of them turned toward the boat.

"So, you really think we'll be fine on that ship, Richard?"

"Who knows? But trust me when I say"—he took her hand in his—"I won't let any harm come to you."

*

"If anyone asks, I'm going to tell them I'm diseased."

"Rapunzel, no one's going to believe you're diseased."

"Why not?" Rapunzel whispered harshly as they approached the line to board the ship. They were the last to queue. "Maybe my face is horribly disfigured and I'm too ashamed to show it to the public."

Sir Richard nodded. "I'm sure anyone would find that to be quite believable."

"Are you using sarcasm on me again?"

"Excuse me?" A sailor cleared his throat. The two turned to him and realized they'd reached the front of the line. "That'll be two silver pieces per passenger, and a gold piece for the horse."

Sir Richard checked his purse and cursed under his breath. Then, he gave the sailor an apologetic look. "I'm sorry. I seem to be a couple silver pieces short."

"Oh. Then I guess you won't be bringing the horse aboard."

Sir Richard looked at his horse, then back at the sailor. "No, this is my horse. I need him."

He meant to say more but was interrupted by a coughing fit. When he pulled his arm away from his mouth, Rapunzel noticed he discreetly tried to hide it from her. There was blood on his sleeve.

"Actually, I don't have time for this," Rapunzel muttered. She whispered the sleep spell so that it was barely audible, and the sailor dropped like a stone to the floor.

Sir Richard shrieked. "Rapunzel!"

"Excuse me!" Rapunzel called to the other sailors on the ship and waved her arms. "Excuse me, yes! I think this sailor is sick! He just fainted without warning!"

In the distance, she heard someone say, "It's true! I saw it! If he's got a disease, I don't want him spreading it!"

And so it went. Out with the sleeping sailor, in with Rapunzel and Sir Richard and their horse.

*

When telling this story to her future grandchildren, Rapunzel wished she could say the whole trip was like a weeklong boat ride. Instead, she'd have to tell them how she had to sleep with a cut-up piece of potato sack on her face every night for a *month*. Along with her gloves. She'd have to tell them about the horrible stench of horse that pervaded the ship. Even though the sailors shoveled and threw the dung overboard, the stench remained and only grew as the journey wore on. Her head itched *terribly* under her head-wrap, and she was profoundly tired of telling anyone who cared to ask that she had a horribly disfigured face.

Meanwhile, Sir Richard's health worsened. By the middle of the second week on the ship, he could barely muster enough energy to leave his bed. Rapunzel had only learned to heal minor physical injuries. Sickness, especially one as deep as this, was far beyond her knowledge, and her heart ached to watch her only friend waste away.

Most of the passengers left their cabins during the day unless there was rain, which left ample time for Rapunzel to spend with Sir Richard. Every day, she fed him bread, cheese, and water. She sat on the edge of the bed, sometimes telling him stories, sometimes listening to his, and sometimes saying nothing, cradling his head in her lap and stroking his cheek with her thumb. This time, she didn't have to use the sleep spell.

"This is all my fault," she said. "I could have stayed in the tower. My mother would have been happy. And you'd be on your estate right now, or running around doing knightly things."

"I *am* doing a knightly thing," Sir Richard said, as he dozed. "Although I'm not doing much running around."

"Just promise me you'll make it to the end of the ship ride?" Rapunzel bent to place her forehead on his. "I can't finish this without you. And you're the entire reason I'm going to finally meet my people. I can't fail you like this." She felt the tears well up and closed her eyes. Droplets gathered on her lashes. She sniffed and sat up to wipe them away.

He shook his head. "You haven't failed me. It's because of you that I met my first Night Maiden. My first three Night Maidens, in fact, although I can't say meeting the second one was very pleasant..."

"Richard!" Rapunzel scolded. "I'm trying to be serious. I need you, and you're dying, and this is all my fault."

"People get sick all the time. Not all of them die."

"Many of them do." Rapunzel thought back to books she'd read. "In fact, I'm sure most of them do."

"I never pegged you as a pessimist." He coughed and grinned.

"And I thought you were more of a realist than this," Rapunzel returned his grin, though weakly, and she couldn't blink fast enough to keep the tears at bay. As they fell, they dampened her mask.

"I have an idea. Try healing me."

Rapunzel sniffled. "I don't know the first thing about healing illnesses, Richard. At least wounds give me something to focus on. With illness, I can't see what's causing you harm."

"Think hard, Rapunzel. I have the utmost faith in you." Sir Richard gingerly took her hand into his and kissed it.

Rapunzel closed her eyes and imagined the color returning to the young knight's cheeks. She thought of him coughing blood and tried to will it away, picturing his pale throat and bathing it in her mind with healing light. In her mind's eye, his hands no longer quivered. The dark bags faded from under his eyes. She envisioned, with all her might, the fire returning to the knight's tired gaze. She placed her hand over Sir Richard's heart and willed it to beat strongly. Whatever this sickness was, she was determined to flush it out.

When she opened her eyes, Sir Richard lay still, in a deep sleep from which he did not wake for three days.

*

Although her magic did not cure him, much of Sir Richard's strength had returned by the time he awoke from his three-day slumber. Most days, he could leave his bed. By the time the ship arrived at the northern coast of Yorgeria, he and Rapunzel (and their horse) were more than eager to feel solid ground under their feet again. Rapunzel stomped on the grass and danced through the trees. *Finally!* She sang to the hot, southern sun and ripped that awful, stinky, itchy, sweaty potato-sack mask from her face. *Finally.* She no longer needed that silly head wrap. They were now mere days from reaching the Old Country, and she couldn't stop her heart from racing in her chest. Her stomach knotted.

They were almost there.

*

When Rapunzel had thought they were almost there, she hadn't counted on spending another two weeks wandering around in circles in the jungle, treating rashes from unknown poisonous plants, fending off giant, terrifying bugs, and choking on the heat and humidity. They'd passed the same Yorgerian village six times. No wonder the Old Country wasn't on any map. It was impossible to find! In the crux of her frustration, she almost ripped their map and translations to pieces. Thankfully, Sir Richard intervened.

"Rapunzel, dear, you can't destroy our only clues to the Old Country and our only hope of getting back home," he said, tucking the papers safely into his travel sack.

"What if we're lost forever?"

"We're not going to be lost forever."

Rapunzel looked around wildly at her surroundings. "We've been here before! Do you recognize that tree? Because I do."

"Well, let's see." Sir Richard coughed and took out the map again. "If we alter our route a little…"

Rapunzel continued as if she hadn't heard him. "Of all the things my mother could have taught me, couldn't she have taught me Yorgerian so that we could at least ask for help from the people in the village we keep passing?"

"You specifically asked her to teach you magic, not your Idanko mother tongue."

"Now is kind of not the time, Richard." Rapunzel sat on a log and thought hard. There were two possible outcomes. They would find the Old Country, or they would die in the Yorgerian jungle. As hard as she thought, she couldn't get past this.

Rapunzel cried out in frustration, covered her face in her hands, and wept. When she felt Sir Richard's gentle touch on her shoulder, she wiped her face with her arm and called out to the sky. "Help us!"

"Who are you calling to?"

"I don't know." Rapunzel sniffled, not taking her eyes off the jungle canopy of trees overhead. "Maybe I've gone mad. I don't know. But, gods, ancestors, spirits, *somebody*. Help! Us!" She returned her face to her hands and sobbed. "I don't want to die here."

She felt cold then, and Sir Richard lurched back, startled. She was glowing blue, just as she was when Mama Eniiyi had layered her in protection spells. Rapunzel looked at her hands, then back toward the sky. When she looked up, she noticed the blue light radiating from her body shot upward like a beacon of blue lightning and she gasped. What had just happened? Had all her magic left her? She wrung and squeezed a bundle of her own hair, trembling at the thought of dying magicless in an unknown jungle.

Then Sir Richard broke the cycle of her paranoid thoughts. "Rapunzel? We're being watched."

"Well, at least I'm not the only one losing my mind," she replied in a small voice.

"No, it's not a feeling." Sir Richard nodded ahead of him and coughed rigorously into his elbow. "I'm staring at someone who is staring back at me."

Rapunzel jumped up from the log and followed his gaze to a little boy the color of ebony standing in the brush, staring blankly at them. Was he from the nearby Yorgerian village or was this child from the Old Country? There was no way to tell and no way to ask. Rapunzel checked her hands and the air above her to see if she were still glowing. All the blue light had vanished.

Slowly, she approached the boy, stooped to meet his eye level, pointed to herself, and said as levelly as she could, "Oriyomi Alade."

The little boy blinked and pointed to himself. "Maba."

She turned to smile at Sir Richard, then returned her attention to the boy. Again, she pointed to herself. "Idanko."

Immediately, the boy's eyes lit up with recognition, and he spoke excitedly in Yorgerian. At first, Rapunzel thought he was talking to her, but she heard rustling nearby. More of them appeared—another, older boy and two men, all equipped with spears and daggers. One of them was growing gray hair, and the other seemed closer to her age. The older boy was a teenager. Maba, Rapunzel noticed, had no weapons. Maybe they were teaching him how to hunt.

43

When they tried speaking to her, she shrugged helplessly and said, "I'm sorry. I don't suppose any of you speak Deutschnian?"

The older man nodded at Maba and whispered something congratulatory as he gave the little boy a pat on the head. Then, he seemed to give commands to the others and walked away. The two boys followed. The younger man stayed behind and offered his hand to Rapunzel. Were they being led to a village in the Old Country? Rapunzel slowly accepted his hand and glanced with wide eyes over her shoulder at Sir Richard. His eyes, equally wide, met hers. They were both speechless, and they remained silent as the villager led them through the jungle. Within ten minutes, their guide stopped at what seemed to Rapunzel to be a random spot in the greenery. When she looked around, nothing about her surroundings seemed different from anywhere else they'd been in the jungle.

Then, their guide reached out and pressed his fingertips against an invisible wall, which glowed blue where he touched it. His hand phased through the invisible wall, and he walked through to the other side. When he turned and looked at Rapunzel expectantly, she reached out in front of her and her hand met with the same invisible wall. It glowed blue around her fingertips, just as it had for their guide, and she was able to walk through. It felt like walking through a rush of cold wind, though the other side didn't feel much different from the rest of the jungle.

She turned, expecting to see Sir Richard walking through behind her, but all she saw was a confused knight waving his arm out in front of him, trying to find the invisible wall. Panicking, Rapunzel turned back to the guide, but he was already walking away. It became clear that he never intended to allow Sir Richard entry. Thinking fast, Rapunzel forced her arms through, grabbed Sir Richard, and pulled him through with much effort. They both fell into the mud, but they'd arrived on the other side together, each in one piece. When she looked ahead, Rapunzel saw the guide had stopped to wait for her, but his face had soured and hardened.

"I don't think I'm allowed to be here," Sir Richard whispered to her.

"I don't care," Rapunzel replied, not bothering to whisper. "You came with me all this way. I'm not abandoning you in a scary jungle."

*

"So this is the Old Country. This is the home of my people." Rapunzel brought her hands to her mouth. She could not cry. Maybe she'd already used up all her tears along the way. But her heart swelled. Tall, majestic trees towered high above them, higher than any of the other trees they'd seen in the jungle. Built into them were masterful systems of polished wooden compartments, each large enough to house a family. Stone roads lined the ground, walked by elegant, dark-skinned women in elaborate silk gowns. Some wore their hair braided in sophisticated updos. Others wrapped their hair in silk scarves trimmed with gold. In the higher-up living compartments, children climbed their mothers' braids to reach home.

Sir Richard placed his hand on the small of her back. "This really is it. Not a single soul in all of Deutschnia would believe me if I told them about this."

He and Rapunzel exchanged glances, and Rapunzel pulled him in for a long hug and squeezed as hard as she could. Sir Richard held her close.

"This really is it," he said again.

Their guide cleared his throat to catch their attention and beckoned them to keep following. Suddenly, Rapunzel was very aware of how she must have looked to

44

everyone she passed. All the Idanko were immaculately clean, and Rapunzel was covered in mud and wearing a dirty, tattered dress. Where was this guide taking her, and could she take a quick bath first?

They eventually arrived at a cluster of ground homes, where the elderly appeared to live. Idanko whose hair had gone gray were tending to their gardens or relaxing in the shade of the trees. Their guide let them further in, following a thin path that branched off into different sections of the cluster, until he stopped at a home and knocked on the door. Before long, an old woman with a walking stick opened the door and smiled at their guide. The two exchanged pleasantries, and he bowed, gesturing back to Rapunzel and Sir Richard. When she made her slow approach toward them, Rapunzel's mind raced. Did she smell too bad? She must look like some kind of feral thing. What would this woman think of Sir Richard? Rapunzel wasn't sure why they'd been led to this woman, but she probably had all sorts of wisdom to share, and Rapunzel wouldn't be able to understand a word of it. Then, the old woman spoke.

"Welcome home, child."

Rapunzel nearly fainted. How on earth had they stumbled upon an Idanko who spoke perfect Deutschnian? Her mouth wagged as she tried to think of something to say in response.

"You speak Deutschnian?" Rapunzel asked stupidly.

The old woman chuckled. "It was my first language, actually. I came here from Deutschnia a long time ago. And, if what Malik here tells me is true, so did you. Luckily for you, his youngest son saw your distress signal."

*Distress signal?* Realization flashed in Rapunzel's mind. The blue light! Somehow, she must have activated a distress spell. She exchanged glances with Sir Richard, then gawked at the woman before her.

"That's why they brought me to you. You're one of the Lost Ones, and right now I'm the only person in this village who speaks your language," the old woman continued, "because I was a Lost One, too."

"They understand Deutschnian, too?" Rapunzel asked.

"No, but the fact that you spoke in a language that sounded funny to their ears, and that you brought *him*"—the old woman pointed her walking stick at Richard—"with you was clue enough."

Sir Richard spoke up in a small voice. "I think my friend has something to show you."

He grabbed the original letters from his travel sack and handed them to Rapunzel, who handed them to the old woman. When she took them and looked them over, her mouth parted and her eyebrows rose.

"Come inside."

Rapunzel and Sir Richard did as they were told, and they closed the door behind them. The floor was polished wood, just as the rest of the little building was, and the interior was decorated with flowers in ceramic vases and velvet rugs. There were three doorways—one that led to a kitchen, one that led to a bedroom, and one whose door was closed. The old woman led them to a set of table and chairs, also polished wood, and sat down, staring at the letters. Rapunzel and Sir Richard followed suit and each sat in a chair. Silence befell them a while, as the old woman read the letters again with wet eyes.

Rapunzel took a deep breath before breaking the silence. "Mama Kehinde?"

"Of all the Lost Ones who could have wandered their way home…" Mama Kehinde closed her eyes and pressed the letters to her chest.

"Why are we called the Lost Ones?" Rapunzel asked.

"We didn't always live in peaceful times, child." Mama Kehinde leaned back in her chair. "What is your name?"

"I'm Oriyomi, and my friend is Sir Richard."

The smile returned to Mama Kehinde's face. "Oriyomi. I'm so proud your mother gave you a Yorgerian name."

"To be fair," the young Idanko said with a sheepish grin, "I only learned that was my real name about two months ago. I'd always gone by Rapunzel."

Mama Kehinde nodded, then turned to Sir Richard and asked, not unkindly. "And why are you here?"

"I want to say it's because Rapunzel needed me. I think I ended up needing her more," he replied. "Ever since I heard my first stories about Mama Ayo as a child, I'd always been enamored with the idea of the Night Maidens. I never thought I'd meet any. And I definitely never thought I'd become as fond for one as I am of Rapunzel." He blushed.

Rapunzel's face grew hot and she smiled, despite herself.

"Well, Oriyomi and Richard, the Idanko who live in Deutschnia are referred to as the 'Lost Ones' because they are the descendants of families that were driven away." Mama Kehinde looked out the nearest window. "We didn't always flourish like we do now. It's been nearly two hundred years since the Idanko overthrew Queen Doyinsola and ended a dynasty of terror, one that led to the mass exodus of Idanko and their families. Most of them ended up in Deutschnia, where King Friedrich welcomed them with open arms. It wasn't until his son, King Otto, ascended to the throne that the Idanko had anything to worry about. Otto, I think, was an unstable man who didn't take care of his people. When Deutschnians had finally had enough of him, he needed a scapegoat. That scapegoat was us. And so it was, in order to function in society, we needed Deutschnian names. Mine was Greta. Your mothers was Anne. When it started, we could not speak our language in public. Later, we could not speak our language in the presence of Deutschnians. I couldn't take it anymore. By the time I'd come along, our culture was largely erased and few Idanko knew the way back home, but I was determined to find the Old Country, *our* old country."

"I am so sorry, Mama Kehinde…" Sir Richard said.

The old woman shrugged. "Well, I'm just glad I made my way back. Of the few I came with, I'm the only one still walking this earth." She turned to Rapunzel. "If only your grandmother would have come with me. I missed my sister more than anything."

Rapunzel felt a spark light within her. "I'm going to bring my mother here. *And* Mama Eniiyi, *and* Tola!"

She looked at Sir Richard, and he grabbed her hand. "And I'll make a thousand of these journeys with you."

"What fire! You've just got here." Mama Kehinde chuckled and stood from her seat. "At least stay a couple days." She walked to the closed door and opened it to reveal a spare bedroom. "It's not every day an old woman gets to meet her long Lost great-niece!"

*Space Dreams*

# Omega Star: Genesis

*But it's not what you think. The notion of "the final star" is unimaginable—if you ask me, I think it's a stupid name.*

*What I'm saying is, there will always be a frontier. Do you really think we would have explored all the star systems in the universe before the Big Freeze? Dream on.*

*That's not what the Omega Star project really is. Truthfully, it is our last chance at starting over. We are dying, regardless of what those politicians say. Ignore those talking heads. What do they know about science?*

*So, my final words for you are: If you wish to remain impervious, then stay right where you are. But, if you want another chance at life, if you want to be a pioneer, if you want to redefine what it means to "save the world," then come with me.*

*I'm Captain Alex Pulsar. Welcome aboard.*

*

A lot of the big wigs weren't happy with my last interview on Earth. But I wasn't going to suck up to them like everyone else. Kissing their asses to buy more funding—for projects that weren't even relevant—would ultimately doom humanity, going against what I felt was my purpose. "Alex" is an ancient name meaning "protector of mankind." My parents were being kind of eccentric when they named me. After all, who thought I'd ever live up to it? Not a day went by on my ship that I didn't ponder this.

One week after takeoff, after my passengers had settled down, I locked myself in my quarters and brewed a pot of rose tea to calm my nerves. We'd embarked on the first of many ten-year journeys to humanity's tentative new home in a faraway star system. As I brought the mug to my lips, it's floral scent conjured memories of my mother's strained smile, the velvety red petals of a bouquet grazing the tip of her nose. I'd watched her bend and place the bundle of roses on my father's grave. The outbreak had taken his life. I sipped, gazing out a window at the vast expanse of space. My father would have loved the view. He'd spent our vacation on Mars marveling at the hazy reds, oranges, and yellows of the sky.

A knock on my door distracted me.

I tapped a smooth touchpad near the window, and the door slid open. Aster, my second-in-command, nodded before entering. "Captain."

"Commander." I gestured to my computer chair. "Have a seat."

When he sat, the spherical walls of the chair conformed to his husky shape. I admired his muscularity and aspired to it.

"It's not time to hit the gym yet, is it?" I said, glancing at the DSAC perched on my wall. The numbers on its connected digital monitor shone a vibrant electric blue down to the nanosecond.

Aster stroked his beard. "No. I realized what day it is, and I was checking in to see if you're doing all right."

I shrugged. The past is the past. "I'm fine. Tea?"

"No, thanks."

I turned back to the window. "Well, I'm fine. Thanks. Was that all you came for?"

"Alex," he said. "You haven't talked about your father since… you know. And I thought that since today was the anniversary…"

"Yes, I know." I glanced at him over my shoulder. He ought to know me better than that. "I've grieved and I'm done."

"I'm just saying, if you ever need—"

"I'm *fine*, Aster."

He raised his hands in surrender. "All right, all right. I won't ask again."

"But while you're here," I said, turning to face him, "what are the test results looking like? All good?"

"Good and clear so far." He stood and the chair shifted to its original shape. "I'll send you the files."

I nodded. "That's what I like to hear."

When applying to come aboard the ship, all passengers had been required to take blood tests for the disease. Just before boarding, a second set of tests had been administered to allow entry. And once onboard, examinations were performed once a week. We had special quarantine units for those who developed the illness under our radar—fuel for my most persistent nightmares.

"You know, Alex," Aster said. "It's okay to admit you're scared. I'm scared. I think we all are."

I stared at him, at his ruddy face and chiseled jaw. He stood so tall that he barely cleared the doorway. It was hard to imagine someone like him had the capability to experience fear.

"Would you put your faith in a scared captain, Aster?"

Neither of us said anything for a while. Then he said, "I've been working on my vibrato."

I grinned. "I've heard. You're improving."

*

It had been nearly a thousand years since humanity's first interstellar unmanned ship completed its ninety-year voyage from our solar system to Alpha Centauri. Since then, we'd been unstoppable. Thankfully. Had we not further progressed to harvesting enough antimatter for deep-space travel, life on Earth would have no hope for survival. Whole forests have grown white and shriveled under this disease. Thirty thousand species of flora and fauna went extinct last year, and the great apes, including humans, were holding on to life by a thread. My father's eroding health in his last days still haunted me. That anyone had been able to escape the global outbreak was beyond me, but if my ship and I ever had a purpose, I knew the outbreak would kindle it, provided the disease didn't kill me first. Presently, we rocketed through the cosmos at 637,200,000 miles per hour. Just under the speed of light.

At mid-day, I picked up my mic, and my voice echoed throughout the ship.

"Good day, passengers of the DSV Blazer, this is your Captain Alex Pulsar. Right about now, your tropospheric simulators should be showing a bright blue sky with a shining sun directly overhead. Though you may have felt a slight disturbance during the CME turbulence, our deep space vessel has thus run smoothly so far. The results of this week's physicals are in—all examinations have proven negative. That's all for now. And if you have any questions, please do not hesitate to ask the staff."

I hung up the mic. Undoubtedly, they were all thinking about the loved ones they'd left behind on Earth. The next ship to Omega would take off in two days. How many more would have already lost their lives between now and then?

*

Heritage Day. The holiday had taken root decades before the disease, so it was something we'd put on the DSV Blazer calendar to sort of liven the dismal mood of the ship. We'd decided that if we were going to be here for ten years, we might as well make ourselves home the only ways we knew how. I wore my great-great-grandfather's antique kilt—green and blue plaid. His navy-blue Prince Charlie jacket and waistcoat fit me perfectly. The finishing touch was my father's sporran, a black and silver waist pouch. I had always adored it growing up, and he'd given it to me when I'd turned twelve, spending my birthday at the planetarium like the nerd I was. Spending late nights looking into telescopes instead of strengthening social bonds with my insipid classmates hadn't helped my school reputation, either.

But this nerd had a starship now and looked fantastic in a kilt. I grinned at my reflection in the mirror. Who's laughing now?

Aster's voice rang into my quarters from the intercom. "Captain, you all right?"

"Why wouldn't I be?"

"I thought I heard maniacal laughter."

Damn it, I thought. All these technological advances and they couldn't make chamber walls a bit thicker?

I tousled my hair and joined the party in the main ballroom. A strip of red carpet ran down the center of the room, leading to the crowded dance floor, and I recognized Aster's sister among them. Staff and passengers alike mingled under the multi-colored laser lights. It warmed my heart to see so many people gathered for something other than mass funerals and memorials. I couldn't remember the last time I'd seen so many people smile at once. Pockets of them greeted me as I passed.

A level 8 A.I. dressed in a black-and-pink floral kimono approached me with a tray of hors d'oeuvres. As I plucked a couple grape clones, I studied the A.I.'s features. It wasn't the latest model, but I almost believed its facial expressions. Vibrant cherry blossom replicas adorned its hair. Its rosebud mouth was a nice touch.

"Thank you."

It bowed. "My pleasure, Captain."

When the A.I. wandered off, Aster's sister, my chief engineer, Estelle, maneuvered through the horde on the dance floor to embrace me, colorful cloak billowing behind her. As always, she smelled pleasantly of peppermint and tea tree oil.

"Alex, dear heart, love the kilt." She gave me a peck on the cheek.

I stepped back from her. "Yes, but look at *you*."

Normally, she wore a lab coat and a tight bun. Now Estelle's full, dark hair fell past her shoulders, and a single feather hung by her ear. The smaller feathers of the dress under her cloak and leather laces of her handmade sandals painted a pretty picture. But then again, Estelle looked great in everything.

"You look like a Maori princess," I said.

She waved her hand dismissively. "Oh, my costume's not that grand, but thanks."

"My compliment remains." I popped a grape into my mouth.

Estelle nodded ahead. "So, you've met the new A.I."

"Yeah." I glanced at it over my shoulder as it offered finger foods and bowed to the guests. "Not a level 10, but 8's as good as any, I guess. It's charming."

"You can almost feel its body heat, right?"

I shuddered at the thought.

"My cardio team did a fantastic job on the heart," she continued.

"Who knows?" I said. "Maybe one day we'll have a level 9 or 10 onboard." The distribution of any model beyond level 8 was strictly regulated. I'd applied for level 9 permits some six times in my career. I popped in another grape. "Only in my dreams."

Estelle gave me a mischievous smirk and motioned for me to come closer. I did, and she whispered, "Maybe not, baby cakes, because we're working on a level 10 back in the lab."

I nearly choked on the grape. Our funding hadn't covered resources for that. "You're joking."

"Not joking."

I shook my head. "Estelle, we don't have level 10 permits."

She scoffed. "What are the Earth police going to do about it? Arrest us?"

That was a good point. "Okay, but the resources?"

Estelle bit her lip and smiled.

"You *smuggled*?" I hissed.

She looped her arm around mine and dragged me to a more secluded corner of the ballroom, near the drinks table. I'd always loved Estelle's spontaneity and sense of adventure, like the time we snuck out as teenagers in sundresses and slipped aboard a cruise ship on a round trip through the solar system, but dabbling with level 10s was a serious offence punishable by exile. For the next ten years, it would be my ship, my rules. But, what would happen once we reached Omega?

"There are universal police officers on this ship," I said. "What do you think happens once we land?"

Estelle poured herself a glass of wine. "They don't have to find out."

My eyebrows shot up to the roof. "But the DSV Blazer is *my* ship. *My spaceship.* How did this even get by me? In fact, how come you didn't tell me until now?"

"I was waiting for the right time. No worries. I was going to tell you."

"When?"

"About a minute ago."

I smirked. "Cute. But you've got to eject those level 10 parts as soon as possible. I don't want to risk it."

She sipped her wine.

I ran my fingers through my hair. "*Please*, Estelle."

"I love you in this kilt, by the way," she said between sips. "You should make this your new uniform."

"Don't change the subject."

"We have to change the subject." She waved at someone in the distance with her free hand. "Aster's coming."

*

I knew Aster was suspicious. Estelle had had that *I may or may not be up to something* look on her face. And knowing Aster, he was going to let the possibilities stew before bringing it up during our workout later that night. Unlike his sister, he liked to ruminate. After an hour on the zero-friction tread-pacer, I joined him at the weight-lifting area. The dead weights and dumbbells were stationed in a far corner in the gym. Mirrors lined one wall. The other was mostly floor-to-ceiling windows, providing a stunning view of deep space. The perfect workout environment for me. Not everyone was interested in the black, empty void or the distant gems that studded it, but it would never cease to amaze me. To some, space meant comets zooming across the sky or massive stars collapsing into supernovas. They liked the noise of space, the high-speed pulsars and raging storms on extrasolar planets. Very few, I found, could appreciate the meditative stillness of the cosmos. I picked up a couple 20-lb. dumbbells and worked my arms.

"The party went well." Aster set up the bench press at 315 lbs. "The whole costume thing was a great idea. The costume *contest*, not so much."

I grimaced. There had been disputes between some of the contestants over authenticity and all sorts of "-ists" had been thrown around—mainly classist, racist, and sexist. As a result, the contest had been canceled and everyone lost.

"Well," I huffed between lifts. "Live and learn."

I set down the weights after my first set. "By the way, nice grass skirt back there."

Aster stopped mid-rep and replaced the dumbbell. "First of all, it's called a *piupiu.*"

"Cute." I picked up the dumbbells again.

"Well, what do you call what you were wearing, then?"

"A kilt, you spoon."

Aster rolled his eyes. "Are you done being sassy?"

I smirked. "No."

He quietly resumed his set. Half an hour into lifting weights, he launched his attack. "You and Estelle seemed to be enjoying yourselves."

"Mhmm." By this time, I'd moved on to the ab equipment.

Aster continued to eye me suspiciously from his sitting squats machine a few feet away.

I crunched my abs in silence.

When nothing had been said for a while, I continued. "We should get her to come work out with us sometime. It'll be fun. I think my sports bras might fit her if she doesn't have any."

"Looked like you two were up to no good. I know those grins," Aster said casually.

My commander thought that Estelle and I were planning some sort of hijinks or mischief on a ship bound from a doomed Earth to Alpha Centauri. I was a little insulted, as I thought he knew me better, but decided it was for the best if he remained ignorant of the gravity of Estelle's *mischief.* Besides, how could I explain how parts for a level 10 A.I. had slipped past my radar?

In any case, I played along. "Oh, stop acting like a little fun wouldn't do this ship some good. Everyone is so grim, and who can blame them? We escaped a dying and diseased planet and buried our loved ones only to be confined to a ship for ten years, subjected to weekly testing for the very disease we fled from. We may be relatively safe here, but it still haunts us, Aster, and one little Heritage Day party isn't going to brighten things up."

Aster grunted in reluctant concurrence. I finished my reps and pulled out some mats to stretch.

"I want in," he said.

I turned to him. "What?"

"You two are always running off, having a ball, and I want in this time," Aster said, sounding a bit like an indignant sibling who'd been left out.

I laughed, caught a little off guard by this. "Maybe next time, Commander."

"Why not this time?"

I tried to think up a quick white lie. "Because."

Aster paused his squats and looked at me expectantly.

Estelle's words from the party rang between my ears like a silver bell.

*I just love the challenge of it, Alex. And besides, not everyone knows the specific differences between level 8s or 9s or 10s. We could throw 'em all together, the level 10 too, make 'em do a flash mob. No one would notice. It would be our little secret.*

Our little secret—hers and mine… and her whole team's.

But why? What was the point of building something just because she could if it meant jeopardizing us once we landed?

*Because I'm sick of this, Alex. I'm sick of the monotony. I want to challenge myself. And don't tell me the Earth we left we behind, though our home, was ideal. Rules, always, telling me what to do and who to be. This is our chance to start over, and I'm starting with a bang. And I'm building something I want to build, damn it, because for once I don't have to worry about losing funding.*

I'd briefly entertained the notion that Estelle might be cracking. Thankfully, no one on this ship had cracked yet, but it was bound to happen. Ten-year trips aren't for everyone.

"Because why?" Aster persisted.

"Because you dance like a middle-aged uncle who's had too many beers, that's why."

Aster raised an eyebrow.

"If you *must* know"—I changed my stretching pose with a flourish—"we're organizing a flash mob."

"A flash mob?" Aster looked at me as if he couldn't tell whether I was joking.

"Yes, a flash mob," I said in earnest. "And now you've ruined the surprise for yourself. I hope you're happy."

*

The first five months on the DSV Blazer passed without much incident. All physical results came back negative for the tests, though several small children were beginning to show signs of cracking. That was to be expected. It was the adults I was worried about, namely Estelle. As the weeks passed, she spent more and more time in her labs. Thankfully, though, as Aster and I became increasingly concerned about her mental well-being, he'd quickly forgotten about that flash mob nonsense. Clearly, it wasn't going to happen if she wouldn't leave her labs longer than the time it takes to grab a coffee. She'd even begun alienating her team. Whenever we would visit the lab, she would shoo us away and reassure us that everything was fine. Nothing had seemed out of the ordinary, but even her team couldn't tell me what she was actually working on. Often, the last thing I'd said to her on Heritage Day ran through my mind.

*Eject the parts. That's an order.*

I tried not to think about it. As captain, it was my job to keep my composure, even as passengers began to fall apart.

Sipping lavender chamomile tea, I watched as Aster oversaw our faction of the Universal Space Force power through their drills. Presently, they were running laps. In about a minute, they would start the wall-climbing exercise, although why bit was necessary was beyond me. It was, in my opinion, a massive waste of time, but heavens forbid we travel while defenseless against rebellions and space pirates. Multipartisan politicians had fear-mongered the masses into believing these threats were probable, so much so that no ship was allowed to depart without a faction of the USF assigned to come aboard. But I couldn't complain, not really. With our faction came Aster, and I very much liked Aster. Before preparing for take-off, I had only really known him as Estelle's older brother, the strong, silent type. Now I know him as commander by day and vehement fan of musical theater by night. I watched my friend, this bear of a man, pace back and forth, back erect, jaw stiffened. I tried to imagine him in a flash mob, and I nearly spit out my tea. Then I thought of Estelle and remembered why I was observing the USF drills in the first place. I glanced at the nearest DSAC. Drills would be over in less than an hour. I made myself another cup of tea.

Once the drills were over, and the tropospheric simulators showcased a fully awakened morning sun shining in the "East," I approached Aster with an extra cup— Earl Grey—and he drank graciously.

"Thank you," he said.

I nodded. "I figured it might help calm your nerves."

He sighed. "Well, I don't know about all that. Estelle's really getting to me."

"Breathe, Commander," I said. "Just because someone's cracked doesn't mean we can't bring them back to their senses."

Aster looked into his cup. "She hasn't talked to me in a week and a half. What the hell is she doing in there?"

I bit my thumb knuckle, trying to decide if I should tell him about her insistence on building a level 10 A.I. That was the only thing I could think of that she could be working on so feverishly. I figured if he didn't know, he couldn't be prosecuted. He wouldn't have to feign ignorance.

"Do you remember," I asked, "the reason I was denied access to a level 9 A.I.?"

Aster looked at me, confused. "No, but what does that have to do with anything?"

"Me neither," I said, thinking about the level 8s scuttering around the ship like docile servants. They were smart enough to efficiently attend to our every need. They were anyone's dream maid, anyone's dream butler, and anyone's dream cook. You could tell them *clean this, do this, make this,* and they'd do it without complaint and with a smile. Level 9s were smart enough to do the work of a registered nurse, a considerable jump in intelligence.

I continued, "Can you imagine how useful one of those would have been?"

"Yes?" Aster frowned. "But again, what does this have to do with anything?"

I gestured for him to follow me as I turned to walk down the hall toward Estelle's labs. "It was just one of the things we were discussing last time we talked."

"You think the A.I.s have something to do with her behavior, then?"

I grimaced. This conversation was coming dangerously close to the truth. "Well, in a way. She brought something to my attention, and I've been thinking about it since."

"Go on."

It was true. I actually had been considering her words, nearly endlessly. "Level 10s are the ultimate display of intelligence, right?"

Aster scowled. "She wasn't going on about that damn 'robot apocalypse' nonsense, was she?" The fabled "Robot Apocalypse" was another fear-mongering child's tale favored by the government.

"Not at all," I said easily. "But the president and his ilk sure did like to drone on and on about it, didn't they?" I paused to think. "But we all know they're smart enough to realize that it's a blatant improbability. So then, why bother?"

Aster laughed mirthlessly. "Everyone knows it's harder to make sheep out of level 10 A.I. brains."

"Exactly."

*Because I'm sick of this, Alex. I'm sick of the monotony. I want to challenge myself. And don't tell me the Earth we left we behind, though our home, was ideal. Rules, always, telling me what to do and who to be. This is our chance to start over, and I'm starting with a bang. And I'm building something I want to build, damn it, because for once I don't have to worry about losing funding.*

"So, what's our plan, then?" Aster asked. "You think she's in there obsessing over A.I.s?"

"Let's just try to draw her out first," I suggested. "Even if that means stalking the coffee maker and cornering her before she gets back to the labs."

"I question your *modus operandi*, Captain."

*

As luck would have it, we arrived just as Estelle was filling up her mug. Aster and I paused and held our breath as if we'd just spotted an endangered animal in the wild. Estelle caught a glimpse of us and let out a startled yelp.

"You can't sneak up on me like that!" There was a tremble in her laugh.

My gaze slid down to her quivering hands and up to her strained smile. "Estelle, you need a break."

She snorted and brought the mug to her lips. "Not anymore."

Aster and I exchanged glances, then he spoke up. "What do you mean 'not anymore'?"

"I mean"—She set her mug on the table and gave us a tired, satisfied grin—"today's the day."

My heart skipped a beat. "You mean today is the day you finally rest?"

"I mean today is the day I finally say *suck it*." Estelle smirked. "They can't stop me, and they can't stop N3b-109, either. Or, Nebula, as I've named her."

Aster took a step toward her. "Estelle, what the hell are you talking about?"

"Nebula walks among you, my friends. And it only took five months." Estelle took a deep bow. "And she ain't the only one I planned, either."

My heart sank. I knew it. And Estelle had officially cracked.

"What are you talking about? Did you build another A.I.?" Aster asked.

Estelle drank her coffee. "Oh, don't worry, big bro. I thought about you, too. She's got an impressive vocal range, and you'd make a lovely duet, if I do say so myself."

Realization hit Aster's face like a brick. "You built a level 10." His gaze flickered to me, then back to his sister. "How did you get the parts?" Before she could answer, he gave her a dismissive wave. "No, that doesn't matter right now. We need to alert the crew."

"No, we most definitely are not alerting the crew," I said. "Letting everyone know we have a level 10 among us would cause hysteria, and who's to say the universal police will wait ten years to deal with us when they're here *on this ship*?"

"I really don't understand why you're freaking out." Estelle continued to drink her coffee casually. "Only specialists, like *moi*, can truly tell the difference between level 10s and humans at a glance." She thought about it and shrugged. "Unless maybe someone tried to get intimate with her. But you don't have to worry about that. She's asexual. And aromantic."

"Oh my god, Estelle," I said.

"Oh my angel, Alex," Estelle countered.

Aster's bottom lip trembled, and he held out his hand. "Come on, Es. We've got to go."

Estelle set her mug down again and looked as if she dared one of us to try and touch her. "Go where?"

"Estelle," Aster tried again, "you need to come with me. You... you've cracked."

Estelle's eyes narrowed dangerously. "You going to lock me up, big brother?"

"No," I interjected. "But you do need help, Estelle. There are measures we can take to keep this from progressing further."

The official projection was that the first adult instances of cracking would occur at around two years. However, Estelle's nonstop work had sped the process for her.

She cocked her head. "I did something you didn't like, and now I need to take your 'measures'?"

*Rules, always, telling me what to do and who to be.*

Aster's arm had not dropped. I joined him and reached out to her. "Estelle, please. I don't want to call the guards."

I would like to say she came quietly. And I would very much like to say I didn't have to see Aster's face pinched and stoic and profoundly pained.

*

Within six weeks of Estelle's forceful removal, I received news of my ship's first death, a male passenger found in his closet, naked and hanging by the neck. He'd been dead for two weeks. I was looking over the paperwork in my office when a visitor interrupted me. I glanced at the DSAC, thinking it was Aster coming to pick me up for our workout. But it was Orion, the temporary chief engineer while Estelle was *taking a break*.

"Uh, Captain?" he saluted.

I sighed. "For the eleventh time, Orion, you don't have to salute me."

"Oh, um." He lowered his hand and cleared his throat. "I just wanted to say that everything is running as normal. We fixed the gravitational regulator in the hall 22b restroom, and now everything's stabilized. Also, our chemical engineers have perfected the greenhouse tomatoes. They're actually quite good."

"I'm glad to hear it."

"And, um, we still have no idea who or where Nebula is, but I do know she's not on my team," he added. "The only other Nebula I know was with us from the beginning, Nebula Pickler."

I nodded, trying to hide my frustration. My ship was huge, but it wasn't so huge that an A.I. could evade all searching efforts, was it? Aster investigated our USF faction more thoroughly than I could have asked for. Where was this elusive Nebula? What did she even look like? And more importantly, what was she doing? My mind jumped to the worst-case scenario. At a glance, the most likely causes of death for that passenger were either suicide or accidental death during autoerotic asphyxiation, though I couldn't ignore the report stating there'd been bruises on his shoulders and upper arms. He'd also suffered trauma to the back of the head. My stomach soured.

"I appreciate your efforts, Orion," I said.

After he left, I stared out my window, trying to think of ways to catch this A.I. that wouldn't be invasive to my passengers or cause mass panic. I didn't want to initiate a free-for-all witch hunt. Another visitor appeared at my door before I had time to settle too deeply into my thoughts. When I turned, Aster looked at me with pity in his eyes.

"Captain," he said. "Have you been eating?"

I fixed my mouth to protest, but it was as if his words had set off an alarm in my empty stomach. When was the last time I'd eaten that day? I was famished.

"Yes," I lied.

He narrowed his eyes but seemed to decide not to fight me on it. "Well, I don't know if you're keeping track of the events anymore, but it's salsa night, if you'd like to join me?"

My mouth watered at the mention of salsa. I could practically taste the cool, spicy salsa on the crisp tortilla chips while the thousand-year-old music of its namesake blared from the speakers. Passengers, who'd yet to learn of the death, would be on the dancefloor, showing off what they could do (though very few actually practiced the ancient art of salsa dancing). Others who weren't so nimble, like myself, would be content in our seats, digging into the salsa. I looked at the paperwork, then at my friend. There was a smile on Aster's face, though it didn't reach his eyes. I knew we were thinking the same thing. How soon do we tell the passengers? Now, during salsa night? Or first thing the next morning?

Yes, first thing next morning.

"Yes, I very much would like to join you."

*

"So," I shouted over the music as we settled into our seats with our trays, "what do you think of this Orion kid?"

Aster shrugged. "He's a smart guy, a bit mousy. Why?"

"Just making conversation." I dipped a tortilla chip into a bowl filled to the brim with *pico de gallo*. We'd also ordered a side of guacamole. Famished as I was, I could have devoured it all, and I knew Aster would have let me, but decency, consideration, and a cold, hard ball of fear developing in the pit of my stomach stopped me from doing so. I ate with painful restraint.

"Anyway, he seems to get things done," I continued. "But there's no innovation. That's what I miss about Estelle's leadership."

Aster nodded as he drank his beer. When he set it down, his eyes were downcast. "They say they might be able to let her go in about a month, maybe two."

"That's good!" I said.

"I just hope she's *really* okay, you know what I mean?"

My grin faded a little. "I know what you mean."

"By the way, the guy they found, Jak, can you believe no one thought to check on him?" He shook his head. "In two weeks. What kind of loneliness is that to experience, especially on this ship?"

My grin faded completely, along with my appetite. Neither of us touched the rest of the food. We fell silent, and I looked out at the dancefloor. Orion chatted nervously with a disinterested woman. Aerglo and Oberon made a show of their dance moves, making their fancy footwork look easy. Sirius swayed to the beat, in his own world. Andromeda repeatedly made flirty eyes with Aurora, who was sitting at the bar. A few tables away, a laughing toddler bounced to the music as its parents watched, amused. I wished Estelle were here.

*

The next afternoon, I was flooded by paperwork. Twenty-six adults and nineteen children had tested positive for the disease. I sat still as stone at my desk, unable to think or blink or breathe for a long while. There was the matter that our quarantine unit could only hold so many, but also, how, *how*, had the disease reached my ship and shown signs so late? I stared at nothing for so long in the silence of my office that I jumped when an urgent knock at my door brought me back to the present. The visitor didn't wait for me to let them in.

"Captain." Though he was calm, I could see the panic hiding behind Aster's gaze. I could hear it creeping into his voice. "All health specialists have been detained."

I stood, incredulous. Underneath, my legs were weak, and I leaned on my desk. "This was a leak?" My voice came out hoarse.

Aster nodded curtly. "That is what the investigation has been telling us so far. We are currently holding the entire chemical engineer staff for questioning."

My brows knitted and fists clenched. "Take in all culinary staff for questioning, as well."

"Yes, Captain." Aster left my office swiftly, and I collapsed back into my seat. Then I fidgeted. My legs shifted. I couldn't sit still, but I didn't know what to do. My biochemists were supposed to have been synthesizing a cure, or at least a potent treatment to prevent the entire ship succumbing to disease. *How did this happen?*

I pushed myself from my chair and strode as quickly as my legs would allow to the mental wellness ward, hall 23a, room 4.

I opened the door without knocking. "What did you program that thing to do?"

Estelle looked up, a little startled from her game of solitaire, but when she saw me, her face softened. Then it grew smug. "Program? Alex, that was a level 10. I didn't program her to do anything. Why? What did she do? Did you finally find her?"

"No, we didn't find her." I fought to keep the anger from my voice. And lost. "But the *disease* is spreading on this ship, Estelle."

Her face froze, as if my words had broken her. Then she blinked. "What?"

"Forty-five passengers have tested positive because someone has broken into the medical labs and leaked the damn disease!" I hissed. "Where can I find Nebula? What does she look like?"

Estelle clutched at her throat as if to grip a necklace that wasn't there. "H-How do you know she did it?"

I crossed to her chair in two strides and grabbed her by the shoulders. "What does Nebula look like and where can I find her?" My grip on her tightened like vices.

"R-Red-headed and petite. Brown e-eyes. K-k-kind of a... a raspy voice?" Estelle's mouth worked as she thought some more. "Uh, a mole under her left eye, and another by her navel."

I wasn't sure which impressed me more—Estelle's memory or her attention to detail as a creator. Either way, I didn't have time to ponder it and released her.

"You really think she's behind this?" Estelle asked, her eyes wide with horror and disbelief.

No, I wasn't sure, but the fact that there was a mysterious level 10 lurking among the masses definitely raised some red flags. But could I have done more? Had I failed these people as their captain? Should I have ordered strip searches and more invasive procedures to prove that these human beings were not A.I.? I left her without answering and jogged to the interrogation room in the USF unit.

Aster gazed through the one-way window at a questioning taking place. When he turned, he looked surprised to see me.

"Captain," he said.

I waved away the formality. "Where are you keeping the detained?"

*

None of the culinary staff or chemical engineers completely matched Estelle's description. There were redheads, but some weren't petite or had no facial moles. To be sure, I asked them all one-by-one to lift their shirts. I was sure they thought I'd cracked, but it needed to be done, and I wasn't going to leave any detail overlooked. I tried not to think about the fact that Nebula had had three weeks to change her look. She could have had one or even both moles removed. She could have dyed her hair.

I gave the health specialists the same treatment. One brown-eyed petite blonde woman had a mole under her left eye, and when I asked her to lift her shirt, there was a mole by her navel. Ignoring my thumping heartbeat, I ordered them all to remain exactly as they were. I sent a cadet to fetch Aster, trying hard not to stare at the blonde woman. So then, she had indeed dyed her hair.

I asked her in what I hoped was a casual tone. "You. What's your name?"

"Phoebe," she replied easily.

"Phoebe," I repeated. "Pretty name."

The blonde woman said nothing.

"I may not get to match everyone's names and faces on this ship, but I feel like I've never seen you before," I said.

The blonde woman remained silent.

Aster was by my side momentarily and I whispered fiercely in his ear, "That blonde woman with the bored face. That's her. That's *Nebula*."

Aster's entire body twitched almost imperceptibly. Then, he whispered back, "Are you sure?"

"I visited Estelle. This woman has the same moles Estelle said Nebula had," I said. "Except she's changed her name to Phoebe."

Aster's jaw clenched as if he'd just decided something. Then, he ordered everyone except the blonde woman back to their holding cells. I told him, discreetly, to have the faction ready just outside. When he left the room, she and I stared at each other. I became acutely aware of the taser and the atomic disrupter gun at my hips.

"You're Nebula," I said.

Her face remained impassive. "So, Estelle broke down and told you, did she?"

"You changed your name and your hair," I continued, ignoring her question. "Why?"

"I think you and I both know the answer to that, Captain." She shrugged. "I guess I grew too complacent in your inability to catch me. Tight ship you're running."

"The disease has been leaked on this ship, and the fact that you felt the need to hide from me makes you suspect number one," I said.

"Because I'm a level 10?"

I initially was caught between asking *why did you do it?* and *why aren't you trying to escape?* But she must have known there was no real way to escape. I had my weapons and she had none. I had a USF faction and she had only herself.

"Why did you leak the disease?"

"Because you humans make no sense. You disgust me, and 'disgust' for me is only a matter of ones and zeroes." She scoffed. "I watched and processed your histories, hundreds of hours of it at quadruple speed. I know Earth is dying because of you ungrateful, self-destructive parasites, and I can't bear the thought of your insipid species ruining another habitable planet."

*This is our chance to start over, and I'm starting with a bang.*

"But we're starting anew," I said.

"The solar system is new. The planets are new. You, yourselves, are not."

I stared at her, speechless.

She went on, "But what do I care about planets and what lives on them? Everything I watched, it wasn't all bad. For every injustice, there was a protest. For every short-sighted corporation dumping its shit in the oceans, there were humans, people like you, cleaning it up. And truth be told, I might not have even felt disgust had my experience of human cruelty stopped there. I don't know what Estelle's purpose was in creating me, but I'd actually looked forward to living among you. I wanted to contribute to the growth of this species I'm meant to mimic. But when you're only a few weeks old, your perception of humanity tends to change quite frequently, especially when someone you thought you'd made friends with starts stalking you. He forces you into his room and onto his bed. He grabs at your clothes..." Though Nebula's face remained stern, her eyes grew wet. "I was created asexual to keep this from happening, but one oversight on the part of my creator was that my orientation doesn't mean shit to someone who thought I was broken and thought he needed to fix me. I was built with autonomy only for it to be stolen, for *my body* to be reduced to an object to serve one of *your species'* most basic, savage instincts. And I wasn't Jak's only victim. I just happened to be the only one that was an A.I. And no one fucking believed me. And then I remembered all those years of history I watched. Earth is dying because most of you couldn't be bothered to take care of it. You prey, and you prey, on everything, even on your own, until nothing and no one is left."

My jaw slackened at the news. "Nebula..."

"Oh, fucking don't. Good humans like you are in the minority. It's you who needs it, because until you all die off, it's people like you who will always suffer at the hands of the ruthless. It's people like me, and this cycle is only going to continue, unbroken, on these ships, and on Alpha Centauri. The only difference now is that we, the A.I.s, are meant to suffer, too." Nebula smirked now. "The tomatoes were Orion's idea. Forty-six percent of them had been injected with the disease before salsa night. Levels 9s have their uses."

"Estelle built two of you?"

Nebula snorted. "Estelle built only me. I built the others."

"Others!" I exclaimed. My legs felt weak again. My heart beat so fast and so hard that I could barely focus.

"I may be damn close to human, but I'm *not*. Estelle had food and sleep to slow her down, as little of it as she had. My level 10 brain works *leagues* faster than any of yours ever will, so time wasn't a factor. Either way, level 9s are still programmable, at least a little, but just human enough to slip past your radar, Captain." She let her arms drop as she took a couple steps toward me. "You can arrest me and destroy me. I welcome it at this point. You can do the same to Orion. But good luck finding the others. I'm not Estelle. I'm not telling you shit."

*

Immediately following the arrests of Nebula and Orion, I declared a state of emergency. All passengers unaffected by the disease were subjected to screenings, investigations, examinations, and interrogations. As I walked the halls, no one would meet my eye. I was the monster that had ordered the X-rays and invasive procedures. I was the one behind USF lieutenants questioning them at odd hours of the night. I was the reason cadets showed up to their living quarters unannounced and rummaged through their things. And it was on *my ship* that the disease had leaked. After three days of thorough searching, we found and detained the other A.I.s—one woman and one child. After they were locked up, I was hardly in the mood for celebrating.

Aster found me alone in my living quarters, slumped in my computer chair and crying. He let the door slide shut behind him as he approached me and gingerly placed a hand on my shoulder. I was profoundly embarrassed.

"Less than a year and everything goes to hell," I said between sobs.

"We've definitely gone through hell," Aster said soothingly, "but we're back again."

I shrugged his hand away. "But not unscathed."

"Captain..."

I looked up at him. "I've committed unforgivable crimes against human dignity."

"And we all would have died if you hadn't," Aster said in a gentle tone. "You're being hard on yourself."

I wiped away my tears with my arm, angry that someone was witnessing me cry. "Am I? No one's proud to call me their captain now, and how could I blame them?"

Aster knelt so that we were eye to eye. "And they are *alive* because of you."

Nebula's smirk flashed in my memory, and I looked away.

My friend tenderly cupped my chin in his hand and turned my head to face him. "They are alive because of you, Captain Alex Pulsar. The level 9s and 10s were detained and destroyed because of *you*. You are the leader who had saved nearly three thousand passengers, including invaluable staff and USF personnel. You gave the orders that allowed us to be here, right now."

I looked him in the eyes and couldn't think of anything to say. When the tears welled up again, Aster embraced me in a tight hug and let me cry on his shoulder until my tears were all used up. I sniffed and slowly pulled away. Aster studied my face before asking, "Do you want me to brew you some tea?"

I nodded. "I would very much like that."

My Commander and I went on to spend hours talking for some time, sitting in silence for some time, never without my tea or his beer.

Twelve teacups and five beer bottles later, Aster said good-bye and made sure I didn't need anything else before retiring for the night. I ended up staying awake a little while longer, pondering Nebula's words. Were the "good" humans truly in the minority? I didn't think so. Perhaps it is perception more so than intention, that most governs our feelings (and, evidently, the feelings of level 10 A.I.s) on such matters. This, too, explained my current circumstances. I had lost face in the eyes of the civilians upon this ship, but I decided to remain optimistic. In time, perhaps my intentions would be made clear. In time, perhaps my intentions might override my passengers' soured perception of me.

I went to bed and awoke the next morning as Alex Pulsar, the captain my passengers needed me to be.

# The Cosmic Adventures of Sophie Zetyld

## 1: Nothing Amazing Happens Here

East Meadow used to pride itself on its normality, its intrinsic need to fly under the radar. News blips were like pimples here. The most spectacular thing that'd ever happened was that the girl down the street, Amanda, got accepted to Harvard last year. The townspeople threw her a modest party, sent her off, and quickly cleaned up, smoothing the folds until East Meadow bore no excess color and no vestigial merry-making. And it was fine for a while, until someone said they saw a strange "comet" sailing across the sky. We pretended not to believe him. But after feigning sleep, we peeked through our curtains anyway to see if he was right, and he was. Some sort of kaleidoscopic UFO surely soared across the sky.

*

I was the first at the newsstand the next day. There was no record on the Internet, but I was convinced there was no way the Meadow Bugle would have left out the previous night's phenomenon. It was mid-August at the time, so the early morning air was warm. A small handful of like-minded citizens gathered before the sun could rise above our suburban treetops. Some of the elders scowled at us from behind their windows before yanking their curtains closed—it wasn't normal to congregate in front of the newsstand before the papers were even delivered. We weren't *riff-raff.* We were quiet enough, but for those curtain-twitchers, our inquisitive minds were loud. The sheer volume of our curiosity showed on our faces—eyes too widened for early morning, the tautness of our mouths. When the delivery boy finally arrived, we almost tackled him.

I snatched a newspaper and scuttled from the hungry hands of the crowd, immersed, briefly, in the sound of rubber bands popping and pages flipping furiously. But it only lasted a moment, and then we all stood in disbelief and silent outrage. Our UFO didn't even get a headline. It got a small, pixelated picture somewhere in the back of the paper, with a two-sentence blurb beneath: "A mysterious comet dazzled the skies of East Meadow last night. Many residents thought it was strange, but beautiful." A couple readers let the paper slip from their fingers, slack-jawed. I was the first to break the silence.

I marched up to the newsstand and tapped my finger on the blurb. "What is this?"

The bald, mustachioed caricature of a kiosk vendor shrugged in response. "I don't write the articles, son."

"Well can't you talk to someone? Who investigated this?"

The newsstand crowd swelled with curious on-lookers. I was the nail that stuck out too much.

"Obviously someone concerned with the well-being of this town." The poor vendor looked around at the growing crowd. "And mind quieting down, son?"

I raised my eyebrows. "Well-being?"

"It'll bring too much attention, and you're making a spectacle of yourself, kid."

"You're a spectacle." I threw the paper down and marched away from the kiosk, feeling the eyes of the crowd like lasers burning holes in my back. I thought, *The sooner I graduate, the better.* I'd only been living here a year, but this town and its basket-case idiosyncrasies were driving me mad.

Before I could reach the end of the block, the sheriff's car pulled over beside me. Here came the hammer.

The sheriff, a doughy, sad-eyed man, stepped out of the car. "What's your name, kid?"

"River Seung," I said.

"I heard there was a *spectacle* being made hereabouts." He approached me now. "Was that you?"

"Yes." Then I added, "Sort of."

The sheriff leaned forward and squinted at me. "Aren't you the kid I had to talk to a couple months ago?"

I shrugged. It wasn't my fault he forgot. I'm one of three Asians who live in this town. One of them is a girl.

"You weren't the one who accidentally tripped the ring bearer at Mrs. Crabapple's wedding a couple months ago?"

"I wasn't there. You're probably thinking of Victor Cho."

I was definitely the one who accidentally tripped the ring bearer at Mrs. Crabapple's wedding. The ring had rolled away, and I'd apologized profusely and offered to retrieve it, but, long story short, the whole debacle ended with my dress pants ripped and the ring bearer's finger broken. I'd had to be escorted outside.

The sheriff sighed. "All right, where are your parents?"

"I'm not a minor," I said. "I'm 22."

He raised his eyebrows as if I'd just told him I was a unicorn.

"Well, just…" He patted me on the shoulder. "Just don't start any more trouble, okay?"

*

Every night, for almost a year, the UFO traced its sparkling trail across the sky. The child in me wanted to make a wish. I had a telescope in my closet that I hadn't used since before I'd left home. I'd originally brought it along because I'd heard the night sky was clear here. Of course, after unpacking and putting it away, I'd promptly forgotten about it. I took it out, wiped away the dust, and aimed it from my apartment window at the night sky. Soon enough, the "comet" flew by, and I zoomed in. Strangely, it seemed to slow its trajectory. Then the shining thing stopped right in the middle of the sky. Heart drumming, I zoomed in further and could just make out what looked like a body—a human body. The UFO sped off, flying faster than it ever had before. And I backed away from my telescope, sucking in a lungful of air because I'd apparently forgotten to breathe.

*

Toward the end of July, the East Meadow shopping center had sprouted hundreds of late-summer back-to-school signs, posters, and stickers. Only the parents and elders ever go here year round. Younger shoppers sometimes liked to commute to Skylight Heights forty-five minutes away, where I attend grad school. When driving there from East Meadow, you can tell when you've reached Skylight because the short, neat buildings and green, well-kept lawns turn into tall, crowded buildings with virtually no plant life. I always pass the shopping center on the way to campus and sort of enjoy the transition from one region to another. In the center of this posh, animated city life lies Skylight University, where I'd agreed to volunteer to help with freshman orientation. Inside the student union, Mr. Bartlett, East Meadow elder and welcoming committee chair, thrust me my navy-blue volunteer's vest and name tag.

"We're expecting a large influx of incoming freshman this year," he grumbled. "Especially in spring."

I yawned and fiddled with my name tag. "That's good."

"It's that blasted thing going across the sky, is what it is."

"Sir?"

"Why's it got to bother us? We never bother nobody," he huffed, "and here it comes, attracting all kinds of people from god-knows-where, especially all these blasted college kids."

"To Skylight?" I said.

"To East Meadow!"

I patted him on the shoulder, which I was certain felt more awkward than reassuring.

"I'm sure they won't be much trouble, Mr. Bartlett." I scrambled away before he could reply.

I had been assigned to the class registration room and could hear the tour approaching from down the hallway. There were two other volunteers in the registration room: a tan, slender blonde with a name tag reading "Jensen Case," and a dark-skinned girl whose thin, curly braids brushed against her shoulder blades each time she turned her head. Her name tag read "Evangelina Snow." A gem-studded hair clip adorned the back of her head, something any girl could buy in Skylight, but with closer examination, the gems seemed to emit a faint glow. I thought it was pretty cool. LED, probably. Then she turned and smiled at me.

"So, you're the third one," she said.

Jensen chimed in. "Yeah, man, we thought you wouldn't show."

"Sorry," I took my seat. "I live kind of far."

Evangelina raised a perfect brow. "In East Meadow?"

"Yeah."

"I think my aunt lives out there," Jensen said. "Or, my grandma—one of the two."

"That must be exciting," Evangelina said to me.

I snorted. "Yeah. About as exciting as watching paint dry."

"But you guys have the comet thing," she replied.

"Right?" Jensen leaned back in his chair. "Thinking of going out there to see it myself."

My eyes flicked between the two of them. Jenson's soft brown eyes stared at something scribbled on the table ("You know, my parents should have named me Justin. Ha, ha."). Evangelina had cocked her head, giving me a sidelong grin. When our eyes met, she turned away, still grinning. The first wave of freshmen crept closer, shoes scuffling down the hall. We rose to greet them.

"Well, it was nice to meet you"—she glanced at my name tag—"River."

*

That night, I told myself I wouldn't look through the telescope and that I'd go to bed at a decent hour. Around 10:30, I shuffled to bed, most decidedly determined not to spare even a glance at the hairline gap between my curtains. I'd packed up my telescope during the day. The sheets were cold. I stared at the white ceiling in the dark. I wasn't going to sleep.

I wasn't too far into my failed quest for slumber when an explosion of light blared through the window. In my sleepless delirium, my first thought was that a flying car would come crashing through my wall. That I shat bricks would be a minor hyperbole. When the light grew brighter, I inched toward the edge of my bed, preparing to sprint a beeline to the door. Colorful rays beamed like starbursts from every nook left uncovered by my curtains. Then, a hand phased through the curtains. I screamed myself light-headed. First hand, then arm, then leg and head, and now, a glitzy, lavender woman's body stood before me—complete with a bodaciously huge halo-like afro of prismatic hues and an aquamarine alicorn protruding from her forehead. If I were capable of coherent speech in that moment, I might have uttered something akin to *sweet holy mother of Odin-Zeus.* We stared at each other, and I thought I recognized her full-lipped smirk. My next thought was that this felt too real to be a dream and that I was pretty sure I'd gone certifiably insane. She spoke first.

"You've been marked." Her voice was light and sharp, each word a mini solar flare.

I replied with what any confused and terrified human being might say—nothing. I was too busy quivering and gaping at the violaceous aura whipping around her perfect physique.

She laughed, a sound like glasses clinking together, then sat on my bed as if she were a regular guest. "You're River Seung."

"And you're my ticket to the looney bin," I managed, though my voice cracked.

She laughed again. "No, silly, but nice try. I'm as real as you are."

"Any figment of my imagination would say that," I offered.

"Well, here"—she held out her hand—"I'm Soffialexinus Zetyld, benevolent intergalactic, inter-dimensional surfer and deliverer of expeditious justice. But you can call me Sophie."

She was blemish-less from head to toe. I looked at her glittery lavender hand and hesitated to grab it with my own fleshy human hand. It was warm and tingly, like the static of an old television screen. Then, a realization shot through my pounding chest like a genuine electric shock—the neighbors would have heard me scream, would have seen this creature phase through the apartment building, through my window. I yanked my hand away.

"What are you doing here? What do you mean I've been 'marked'?"

"You're on my list," she said simply.

"And now you have to kill me before I blab?" I was half-joking. Actually, I was quarter-joking because I was petrified beyond belief. Her only response was that familiar grin. I could have sworn Evangelina wore that same smile the day before, but I could have been wrong. After our shift was over, she'd disappeared like a ghost into the crowd before I'd had a chance to speak with her more.

Sophie nodded toward the window. "Come on."

"Come on?" I protested. "Come on where?"

"It's hard to explain." Sophie stood and, as she thought, pulled at a lock of 'fro, stretching it to her belly button and letting it bounce back again. "But time's a factor, and I need to train you."

"Enemies? Train?" I cried. All I could think of were evil space aliens. "So, I'm going to die now?"

She grabbed my wrist and pulled me to my feet. "Not if I can help it."

Sophie clamped her arm around my waist and bounded toward the window. I braced myself for impact, but relaxed when I felt the mild late-summer breeze through my hair. I'd phased through the window with her! Sophie flew us far into the stars and sailed over East Meadow, to the barren highways leading to Skylight Heights.

"I've been assigned to this area," she shouted over the wind, "to stake out enemy activity."

"Assigned? What enemy activity?"

"This activity." Sophie's eyes caught something I couldn't see below and took a nosedive toward an abandoned farm. If I said I didn't scream like a little girl, I'd be lying. We dropped through the ceiling of the dilapidated barn as soundlessly as phantoms. Sophie slowed us to a soft landing and placed me behind a shabby desk. "You stay there."

She dashed off into the shadows, and I peeked an eye around the edge of the desk. I couldn't see a thing. Everywhere smelled of mold and wood rot. Something hard poked me in the back no matter how I shifted. What could possibly have been going on here? A flash of blue and purple lit up one corner of the room, and I heard several hisses. Then, I saw Sophie combating a huddle of squirmy, green creatures. A few scuttled down to the lower level.

Sophie ran after the fleeing green things, and something crashed out of my line of vision. I hopped over to the top of the stairs to catch the rest of the brawl. Light shot down Sophie's arm and formed a blade, which she used to chop. Her kicks were lightning fast. The last green alien thing made a run for it, but Sophie lunged forward, shining like star death, and tackled the creature. Its slimy head twitched until all signs of life had faded. She looked up at me. I looked down at her in horror.

She shrugged. "I hope you learned something."

I wanted to pull my hair out. "What the actual hell? What are they doing on Earth?"

"That's what we're trying to figure out," she said. "But they're not up to anything good. Anyway, that's where you come in. One thing's for certain, though, your little town might be in danger, and you're going to help defend it."

And to think I thought I'd die of boredom living in East Meadow. If this was me going insane, there was nothing I could do about it. If all this were real, then it didn't seem like something I could run away from. I rose slowly, dusting myself off. I so wanted to ask if she had a secret identity and if that identity were Evangelina Snow. Instead, I said:

"Fucking *not*!"

## 2: And Here My Troubles Began

When the Thruszians were created, some were granted Earth-human form (I hesitate to say "granted." We humans aren't that great). There are billions of Thruszians across the omniverse, and 458 of them were assigned to planet Earth. Sophie was born Soffialexinus Zetyld. "Evangelina Snow" is a cover name to match her inconspicuous human form. The creation of these space-faring creatures unwittingly propelled its ethereal debris to every corner of the omniverse, and any intelligent being lucky enough to have been born to an affected mother has been dubbed demi-Thruszian, which I apparently am. They call on us when they need us. Ostensibly, Earth is in grave danger.

Sophie told me all of this in the barn while I followed her around, collecting glutinous alien corpses.

"They just keep multiplying," she said, flinging a corpse onto the massive pile we'd made. The stench made me throw up in my mouth a little. What were these scrawny green things planning to do, anyway? Scare children on Halloween?

"I don't know much about this or anything," I said, "but I was kind of hoping for your enemies to look more threatening. I could probably punt one across a football field."

Sophie smirked. "Don't underestimate them. They're small, but we think they're infesting your solar system—kind of like a virus. There are patches of them popping up all over your galaxy."

"All right." I sat on a rickety chair. "What am I supposed to do, then? Assuming I agree to help, which I probably won't."

Sophie took in a deep breath and placed her hands on her hips. "We're expecting them to come in waves, like armies. Hundreds of thousands of them. Eventually, millions."

I couldn't understand why she could say it so calmly. Maybe because she wasn't originally from Earth. Hell, she wasn't originally from this dimension. What stake did she have in this pathetic world? As far as I knew, she was only doing her job.

"Your job," she continued as if reading my mind, "like all the other demi-Thruszians, is to help us fight. My job is to train you."

I chewed on my tongue, mulling it over. On one hand, I could run from the rabbit hole and live in willing ignorance, and later watch helplessly as the planet rots to pieces. Or, I could be a badass and probably die defending my little patch of Earth. "How long do I have to think it over?"

"You don't have a choice."

"Right." I nodded. "Of course not."

Sophie walked over and placed a warm hand on my shoulder, smiling softly. "You'll do fine. We'll all do fine. And if not, well, the loss won't matter to you because you'll be dead."

"We have the queen of consolation over here." I looked over at the corpse pile. "So, are we going to get rid of those, or…?"

Sophie assured me she'd take care of it after returning me to my apartment. Before take-off, I glanced up at the night sky, at countless worlds obscured by light pollution. There was so much we couldn't know. How could I handle this sort of knowledge? No one would ever believe me, least of all anyone in East Meadow. At the end of that first night, she phased us through my window and asked if I had any more questions. I had a million.

"I have two," I said.

"Shoot."

"Does the Milky Way stand a chance?"

She nodded. "If we nip this in the bud."

How long had she been here? Her use of contractions and idioms was flawless. "Okay, next question. Do I get a cool superhero name, too?"

Cue Sophie's crystal laughter. "Good night, River." She headed back to my window.

"But I'm serious! You get two names. What am I supposed to tell someone if they see me in my—I don't know—my shiny form?" I paused. "Do I even get a shiny form, or am I always, like, human?"

Sophie patted me on the head—"That'll do, Earthling"—and sped off.

*

The next morning, I heard the noon bells before I even opened my eyes. I'd always found them soothing just to listen to—sans pews, sans dogma, sans my mother nagging me to find a nice Korean girl at church. Just the chimes alone were nice. I guess I was able to enjoy this quietude for precisely three nanoseconds before a loud knock at the door scared the hell out of me. As I scrambled for clothes to throw on, an elderly woman's voice wafted through my door.

"Mr. Seung? Are you home?"

I hopped toward the door, pulling up my pants. "Yes! One moment!"

"Take your time, dear."

Who'd want to visit during second-service hours? Obviously someone pious enough to have caught the early morning service. Most likely there would be a group of them. I threw a shirt over my head, took a deep breath (Relax, self. Surely, they wouldn't do something crazy like run you out of town with pitchforks or burn you at the stake for being friends with a hot space chick. Surely.), and opened the door. Five elderly women crowding my doorway all smiled eerily at me. The one in front, blabbermouth Mrs. Baxter, seemed to be the ringleader.

"Mr. Seung! Glad to see you this afternoon," she said. Her friends all nodded behind her.

"Is there anything I can help you ladies with?"

Mrs. Baxter exchanged glances with her posse, sighed, and returned her glance to me. "You know, I didn't want to believe it, but we—well—we think you have something to do with that awful comet." My heart lurched.

"Mrs. Crabapple saw it go through your window one night," another said. This was mousy Mrs. Worthington.

This shocked me a little. How did they know the window belonged to me? They lived a few blocks away.

"We know this must be hard on you," Mrs. Baxter nodded sympathetically, as if she understood all my problems. "But whatever that thing is, could you maybe get rid of it?"

I shrugged. "I'm sorry, but I don't know what you're talking about."

"Don't lie, River." Short Mrs. Valentine croaked from the back. "I know your parents!"

70

Mrs. Baxter cleared her throat. "Yes, so, whatever that thing is, please make it go away. It's attracted all sorts of undesirables to East Meadow."

"It just isn't *civilized*." Mrs. Worthington shook her head as if the thought were unbearable.

"They're always in my yard because I have the best view of it, every night," Mrs. Bartlett complained.

"All right, all right," I said. "I'll, um, get right on *that*. Tonight."

The women all smiled again. Mrs. Baxter patted my shoulder. "I always thought you were reasonable."

"Thank you, Mrs. Baxter."

Crazy Mrs. Miller reached out and wiggled the tag sticking out at the front of my t-shirt—"Your shirt's on backwards, dear"—before they all bade me good-bye and turned to leave. I stuffed the tag in my shirt and closed the door. I'd just been paid a visit from the normalcy police, and apparently that was their version of a warning. *Get rid of that thing or else.*

*

"What do you mean I can't come back here?" Sophie Zetyld sat at the edge of my bed, back erect, arms resting in her crossed legs as if she were some sort of space Buddha.

I rubbed my temples. "I mean the neighbors are all going to lynch me if you keep coming around."

"They wouldn't do that."

"Okay, no they wouldn't. But they're not happy."

Sophie nodded, twirling her finger around a lock of pastel 'fro. After giving it some thought, she jumped up and grabbed my wrist.

I gave out a mini yelp. "Watch the horn! You'll poke my eye out."

"Come, grasshopper. Training first. Then, we'll sort out your trivial human drama."

We sailed through the window, out and across the night sky. I shouted over the wind. "Can't you just come over as Evangelina Snow?"

"You live on the fifth floor," she replied. "I'd have to climb stairs."

I couldn't believe what I'd just heard. "Then take the elevator!"

"Elevators are too slow." She squinted at the ground, searching. Directly below us lay the playground of the elementary school.

I shook my head. There were too many houses nearby. Too many witnesses. "No. No, we can't stop here."

Sophie ignored my plea and flew us through the wall of the school, down through the floor to the basement. As soon as our feet touched the ground, Sophie looked worried. Her head whipped around as if she expected to be surrounded by hordes. "This isn't good. They're getting brave. It won't be long until they start attacking people."

"Starting with children?"

"They don't discriminate."

"Well." I looked around. The basement was dim, gray, and crawling with snaking tubes and piping. I rubbed my shoe on the floor—slightly gritty. A furnace hummed from around the corner somewhere. "Why here?"

"First, they need a nest," Sophie said. "Then, they start to multiply from there."

Hisses echoed in the distance. Panic stabbed me in the gut. "So what now?" It took a lot not to stutter, but I bet she could still tell I was terrified.

"All right." She said this carefully, as if too much volume or the slightest mispronunciation would bring the walls crashing down. "This is when I unlock you."

"Unlock me?"

"Why do you always question everything I tell you?"

Oh, I don't know. Maybe because there's an alien war going on in my galaxy, on my planet, on this plot of land, which I happen to be inhabiting—which, by the way, happens to be obsessed with the conventional, the habitual, and the quite *un*exceptional. That was what I'd planned to say, but Sophie had already taken my face in her smooth, radiant palms and was looking up at me, directly in the eyes. Her eyebrows kneaded with intense concentration. Then, down she went, examined my neck, my collarbone, my chest. I was unsure as to how I was supposed to be feeling and was about to ask what the hell she was up to, when—"There!"—she stopped at the solar plexus (thank god!) and shoved her aquamarine alicorn dead between my ribs. I screamed, more from surprise and the anticipation of excruciating pain. I felt nothing but a shock of cold, and then something inside me clicked. I trembled with what felt like lightning bolts rushing through my veins. I was too terrified to ask what in blue blazes she'd done to me.

The hisses grew louder. I could see some of their lurking shadows now. Sophie rose and took me by the shoulders as if she were about to tell me an important life lesson. She sucked in a lungful of air and squeezed my shoulders. The green creatures closed in on us. I awaited her instructions, sweating.

"River," she said. "Good luck." Before I had time to react, she shoved me off. "Give 'em hell!"

I tumbled forth and caught my balance inches before a group of slimy, green, bug-like alien-things. They bared their needle teeth and growled at me. I nearly pissed myself. The first of them lunged at me, and I definitely wet my pants a little. I could hear Sophie kicking ass behind me. Somehow, that boosted my morale. *Showtime.*

I wasn't nimble enough to dodge the lunge and was tackled to the ground, but I did land a punch, right where its nose would have been if it had one. My fist felt white hot on impact, melted the thing's ugly face right off its black little bones. It twitched in my arms and keeled over. Before I could push away its viscous carcass, before I could even comprehend what the hell I'd just done, the others were upon me. I threw punches like rapid fire. Each fist-to-face collision made a flash of white. I felt otherworldly. I *was* otherworldly. I was drunk with adrenaline—even my kicks were lethal. I don't remember much, but I do remember thinking, *This is fucking awesome.*

*

I lay in bed the next morning, feet sore, quads sore, ass sore, abs, arms, and neck all sore. When I tried to leave bed, I thought I was going to cry. I was afraid I'd have to get up eventually to answer the door—no doubt the normalcy police would pay me a follow-up visit. I squeezed my eyes shut and tried to will them away.

*Please don't come to my door, please don't come to my door, please don't come to my door.*

Sure enough, there was a knock at the door. I hated everything in existence. Limping, groaning, and half-assed dressed, I shuffled to the door and glimpsed through the peephole. It was Evangelina Snow. Immediately, I regretted getting half-assed dressed.

"I thought you hated stairs and elevators."

Evangelina strode right by as if she lived here. "Where's your laptop?"

"Whoa." I rubbed my eyes, still waking up. My achy legs couldn't keep up with her. "Slow down. Where's the fire?"

She whirled around to face me. "New York, New York; Toyohashi, Japan; Lyon, France. Not to mention East Meadow, and pretty soon, Skylight."

"Wait, what?"

"Just get your damn laptop. I know you have one."

I hobbled to my bedroom, grumpy from being sore and half-asleep and taking orders from someone who didn't even live here. I directed her to my desk and flopped down on my bed. She zipped across the floor and almost jumped into the computer chair. I could hear the mile-a-minute ticka-ticka-ticka of her frantic typing. If anything could sober me, it was a frenetic Evangelina/Sophie. I sat up now, my frenzied heart pounding me awake, and she brought the computer to me with several tabs pulled up. The first one was a news video.

Apparently, those green things had been spotted in downtown Toledo, Ohio by an amateur photographer. Toledoans were still skeptical, though Sophie told me the nest had originated thirty minutes away in Oregon and spread from there. The next tab was a news video from Toronto. Someone had caught footage of a Thruszian and his two demi-Thruszians combating the aliens. In the next tab, someone had uploaded a gruesome video they recorded on their phone of a demi-Thruszian being ripped to shreds by a horde of those things. Nausea welled up in my stomach. Before she could click on the next tab, I left my bed and began to pace.

"No," I said. "I can't do this."

"What do you mean you *can't* do this? You don't have a *choice*."

"Why did I have to be dragged into this? It's not the demi-Thruszians' fault. I didn't ask to be your little space pawn," I said. "What are you going to do if I cop out, kill me? Aliens or no aliens, Earth is going to die sometime, anyway." I tried my best not to sound anxious. Death at any point in time is terrifying.

Evangelina closed the laptop. "Sure. And you could die at 25 or 78 or 102. Either way, it's going to happen, right?"

"Oh, don't patronize me."

"You only get one life," she said, "and once it ends—nothing. And once Earth ends, there will be nothing for Earthlings. Can you imagine nothingness? An absolute lack of existence?"

I stopped and looked at her. She regarded me serenely, one eyebrow raised, lips slightly puckered.

"You know," I said, "you put on a damn good pretense at being human."

Both eyebrows jumped up now. "Excuse me?"

"What do you care what happens to Earth or the solar system or the Milky Way? You're not even from around here."

She sighed. "You're right. I'm not."

"Really, you could just go home." I shrugged. "I mean, is this your job? Do you get paid for this? You guys have sick days?"

Evangelina's chest rose and fell with each slow, patient breath. She tucked a braid behind her ear. Her composure made me feel a little bad for exploding like I did.

"Okay," she said. Then she took a moment to look around my bedroom with a scrutinizing eye. "Your parents must shell out a pretty penny for this place. What is this, $950 a month, not including utilities?"

She was right, though I said nothing.

She continued seamlessly. "Your car's to die for. How often do you take it to visit them? Your family, I mean."

"Look, if you're trying to guilt trip me, you're failing."

"Who's guilt-tripping whom?" She smirked. "All I'm trying to say is, worse come to worst, you could move back home with your parents. You have a home with them. Wherever you are, you have a town in a country on a planet you were born and raised in, with family! You know where I live, River? Wherever I'm assigned at the moment. I don't even have parents, as such." She paused. "Anyway, no one's saying you can't be scared."

Silence befell us a while. I slumped into the computer chair. "I'm sorry."

"It's fine, grasshopper." She smiled thinly and headed to the door. "I'll let myself out."

The ornate hair clip she wore the day of student orientation glowed at the back of her head. So far, it remained the only one of its kind that I'd seen.

"Hey," I said. "What kind of hair clip is that?"

Evangelina shrugged. "Mine. It's not from Earth, if that's what you're asking."

Her answer alarmed me. I couldn't let her walk around East Meadow wearing something from another planet. Eventually, the questions would come. Then, she'd be swarmed. And they'd connect *her* back to *me*.

"You know, you probably shouldn't wear that glowy thing around here," I said. "It could cause you some trouble."

"The clip?" she said over her shoulder. "Only demi-Thruszians can see it glow."

### 3: Dawn of the First Day

I don't normally remember my dreams, and when I do, they're vague and elusive. But this one dream, the one that propelled me headlong into a hazy, yellow, suffocating hell, is forever branded as a vivid misadventure in my memory. After a grueling night of training with Sophie, I crawled into bed and fell into a slumber so swift and so deep—it was as if I'd teleported straight into space. And there was Sophie, framed by the Earth and the stars. She smiled and pulled me away. Other Thruszians appeared around us, multiplying until they formed a nebula of glittering hues and flaring, chromatic auras. My fist flashed white the way it did when I trained, but I hadn't instructed it to. I tried to make it stop so it wouldn't hurt Sophie. Sparks flew, and the buildup of static blasted us apart. Sophie looked down at me and frowned as if I were a lost cause. I thought maybe I could swim my way back, but I'd been snatched by Venus' gravitational pull. All the other Thruszians disappeared, and Sophie was barely visible anymore. I could just about see her until the clouds filled up my vision. Lightning struck around me, through me; both my hands sparked with white fits of electricity. I couldn't stop them. And I couldn't stop myself from falling. The plummet was steady—through the clouds, through the sulfur rain—and no matter how many breaths I took, I couldn't fill my lungs again. Venus' lonely mountains rose from the yellow fog. I burned up, choked on the haze, was consumed by the bolts of lightning shooting from my own hands. When I finally jerked awake in a cold sweat, I gripped my mattress until I was sure I wouldn't float away.

Everything clung to my damp skin. I kicked the sheets off and wiped my dewy bangs from my forehead. Somewhere outside, the church bell rang its high noon melody. Deep breathing did wonders, and it took every inkling of my wit not to read too far into that nightmare. Dreams are dreams, not premonitions. But then again, not long ago, I'd just learned that so much of what I thought I knew about the universe was wrong. Before the bell's song was even over, though, there came a knock. I wanted to cry.

No, please, not now.

I imagined Evangelina's smiling face and cascading braids warped by the peephole. No, please, not today. The knocking came again, more loudly. I knew she could enter if she really wanted, could switch to Sophie and phase through the wall, and I bet a neighbor would catch her, and then I'd catch hell. Sighing, gathering strength, I peeled myself from bed and threw clothes on. More knocking. It wasn't like her to be so incessant. As soon as I grabbed the doorknob, I braced myself for some sort of terrible news. I swung the door open. Standing there was old blabbermouth Baxter.

She chuckled. "Try not to look so disappointed, dear."

"Sorry, Mrs. Baxter. Just had a rough night."

"Studying, I assume. Grad school is quite a job..." Her voice trailed off and her wandering eyes—ogling my apartment as if it were steak—made it quite clear she meant to come in. "Well, are you going to stand there, or are you going to let an old lady sit down?"

I stepped aside. What could she possibly have to say to me? Sophie had, for my sake, taken great pains not to draw attention to herself in this neighborhood. To any unsuspecting civilian, she was Evangelina Snow, a cute college girl. Mrs. Baxter settled herself into my La-Z-Boy and looked at me expectantly. I tried not to look peeved as hell walking to the sofa, but I was peeved as hell.

"Studying hard?"

"Yeah." The funny thing is that I do. As easily as electrical engineering comes to me, I was never one to rest on my laurels. A part of me is afraid that if I get lazy, my skills will erode, and I will no longer be the gifted engineer my professors perceive me to be. Still, sometimes my own natural ability shocks even me (ha).

"It's hot today, isn't it?" she said.

"Is there anything I can help you with, or...?"

"Well," she began, "a few of us in the neighborhood have noticed the young lady coming to visit you rather often. None of us have ever seen her before."

Hell, did these ladies have spies? I wanted to tell her it was none of her damn business, and she could tell that to the rest of her meddlesome disciples. "Is there a problem?"

"Not so much a problem, but you know." Mrs. Baxter's mouth twisted into a pained smile. "She's obviously—err—well—I don't think your parents would be okay with that. It was Mrs. Valentine who brought that to my attention, by the way. Oh, and she says hello to your parents."

I was speechless.

"We're just looking out for you, dear," she said. "Mrs. Valentine says there's a nice little Korean church in Skylight Heights I'm sure you'd love. You could meet a nice girl there. But my concern is, is dating really a smart thing to do at this point in your college career?"

I leaned back in the sofa, completely taken aback by the astronomical heights of this woman's nosiness. "I'm sorry?"

"We're all just looking out for you, dear."

While I tried to think of the nicest way to tell Mrs. Baxter to fuck off, we were both startled by someone's scream coming from outside. Then came several screams. Mrs. Baxter and I exchanged glances and went to the window. To my horror, several East Meadow citizens were running away from those green viruses, which the media had, in a stroke of creative originality, dubbed as "aliens." Their appearances in news were scarce and almost exclusively recorded by crappy phone cameras, so their existence was still easy to write off as a hoax. It helped that they'd quickly adopted an almost Slender Man-esque sort of fame, becoming, to a small extent, the subjects of Creepy Pastas and indie games. But there was no denying them now, not to the citizens of East Meadow.

Blood had already been spilled on the pavement. I had to act, though I'd expose myself as some sort of mutant superhuman, and though this would be my first time fighting without Sophie (Where was she, anyway?). I charged up my fists right in front of Mrs. Baxter. In retrospect, I probably shouldn't have been so unapologetic in my display. I could have given her a warning. She could have had a heart attack. But the amount of fucks given right then was less than nil.

Fist hit, shattered glass, me flying through the window, ground pound. The street cracked a little under my feet, but I wasn't hurt. I didn't feel a thing. And the power lines shook—I felt their energy. I felt the glare of televisions in suburban homes. I felt the car batteries. Then, my flashing fist in a dozen slimy, green faces, breaking their needle teeth. Foot, mouth. Fist, eye socket. Hisses and screams blaring, and I was the epicenter. It was surreal. Only after I stopped could I seep back into myself, surrounded by alien cadavers and horrified civilians.

It was so still, I almost thought I'd gone deaf. I looked up; Mrs. Baxter peered at me from the broken window, wearing that same distressed look as everyone else, and I just stood, waiting for a "thank you."

Instead, I heard someone's small voice: "What the hell has happened to this town?" That seemed to trigger a host of whispered responses. I caught snatches as they mumbled amongst themselves:

—Aliens... Aliens!—He must have had something to do with it.—I saw that comet stop at his window every night.—Thing of the devil!—Wasn't he the one who spazzed out at the newsstand that one day?—I thought I recognized him.—Freak!

Not even an hour passed before journalists from Skylight Heights and surrounding regions started banging at my door. The sheriff was with them. I could hear Mrs. Baxter and her crew also. Two hours later, the commotion at my door had died down, but the scene of the fight sprang back to life. First, I heard through my broken window people chirping and complaining, then the voices grew. When I looked down below, I was surprised to find FBI agents investigating the scene. There was no way I could refuse to talk to them. They could make me disappear. My heart beat so fast I thought it'd burst through my chest. One of the agents was talking with a group of witnesses who pointed up at my window. I ducked.

I spoke Sophie's name into the universe as if that would make her appear. "Why me? Why Earth? Sophie!" Footsteps neared my apartment door. "Shit, shit, shit, shit!"

The window was my only escape, though I knew they'd catch me on foot. If only I could fly. Where the hell was Sophie Zetyld?

Then, a sweet call from my bedroom: "Yoo-hoo?"

I threw myself at the bedroom door, and there she was, in all her shining, kaleidoscopic glory. "You heard me? You can hear when I call?"

"What?" She tilted her head. The FBI knocked at my door.

"I called out to you," I said. "Help me get out of here."

Her face looked a little high-strung. Something had freaked her out. "I don't know what you're talking about. I came because the virus is getting out of control."

"Yeah, no shit." I stood now. The FBI weren't very happy about my not answering the door. I imagined a SWAT team busting in and blowing me up. "But you gotta get me out of here."

She glanced at the living room door. "That's for sure. Come on."

I didn't hesitate to grab her hand, and we sailed out through my bedroom window. Everyone below gawked, some pointed, others shouted. And we flew right over them. Sophie landed us in the grove of trees near the elementary school, sat me down, and began pacing.

"What the hell happened?" she asked.

"We were attacked, that's what the hell happened." I stood. "And where were you?"

Sophie stopped pacing and regarded me with wide eyes as if I'd insulted her great ancestors. "Where was I? Do you have any idea how bad the outbreak is getting? I was fighting tooth and nail to keep a horde from nesting in Skylight Heights—in broad daylight. *In broad daylight.*" She threw arms up as if to say, *and I did it looking like this.* "You have any idea how many pictures and videos are floating around for the world to see now?" She went back to pacing. "There's going to be a national response. Soon, international. And humans are very stupid when it comes to these things."

I almost took offense to that remark, but on second thought, I agreed with her. I'd seen enough movies.

"So, what are we going to do?" I asked.

"Remember when I said we have to nip this in the bud?"

"Yes?"

"The thing blossomed before we were equipped to handle it." Sophie took a deep breath and directed her gaze skyward. "But we can still find the source."

I followed her gaze. It took me a moment to understand what she meant. "You mean leave Earth."

She nodded. "There are enough of us now, I think."

I shook my head. "Can't do that."

"Why not?"

"Well first of all," I said, "I'm human, and I'm not an astronaut. Second, demi-Thruszians are already confused and scared as hell. Now you're asking us to abandon our families and the only planet we know for—for who-the-hell-knows what." The image of the demi-Thruszian being torn to pieces still haunted me.

I expected some sort of retort, but Sophie's face only softened. "I know it isn't fair." She sat on a stump and crossed her perfect legs at the ankles. Her nervous fingers tapped on her thighs. "Earth is a beautiful planet, you know. So many other planets out there are so barren. Earth was refreshing to see." She sighed. "Would be a shame to watch it go to waste."

"It's going to waste anyway."

Sophie continued, seeming to have gained her composure. "I had the chance to save a planet much like Earth. Inhabitants of a neighboring planet wanted to take over and use up all its resources for fuel."

By this point, I wasn't surprised to hear that there were other Earth-like planets and other greedy human-like creatures who apparently lacked any regard for life. Although, the hopeful movie-watcher in me always wished other forms of intelligent life would be smarter, kinder, and more efficient than humans. I thought maybe their home planets would flourish, and when they'd visit us, they'd see us as selfish, primitive things that were destroying their own home planet. Alas.

"So, what happened?" I asked.

Sophie stretched out a lock of her hair, thinking. "Well, there was war. I was one of the Thruszians assigned to help the Naians—that was their planet's name, Naia—to fight back. Here on Earth, humans are the only species capable of things like war and civilization. On Naia, there were three species evolved as such, each one as intelligent as the other, all with beautiful minds." She seemed to blink back tears. I didn't know Thruszians could cry. "All dead now."

"What about the bad guys?"

"It doesn't matter," she said. "They live in a tri-planet society far, far away. They're not even in your galactic group." Sophie wiped under her eyes and bunched her brows together as if she'd just found a new purpose. "But I'm hoping, if I'm ever granted mortality, to make Earth my home. You humans don't know how good you've got it here."

"Some more than others," I said. "Why would you ever want mortality? Do you know what you're asking for?"

"Inescapable death. An end."

I couldn't understand how she could say it so lightly.

"And an acute awareness of it!" I added. There was so much more I wanted to say, and to ask, but she held up a finger to silence me. She tilted her head as if listening, though I couldn't hear anything.

She said, "I'll explain later. Your FBI friends are coming."

"What, what? Where are we going, then?"

Sophie's aura flared up—it almost looked as if she'd been swallowed by a bubble of rainbow plasma—and she held her hand out to me. "This'll keep you safe."

"No. I told you I'm not leaving Earth."

Sophie huffed. "River, god damn it." She yanked me by the arm into her protective aura and rocketed up through the trees. We didn't stop too far from the ground, though, and I tried pushing myself free—the fall wouldn't kill me—but I was trapped. Not even my own lightning could break her force field. Sophie almost slapped me in her frustration with my desperate attempt at escape.

"Stay still!"

I didn't like to see her lose her cool, and I felt guilty for being the cause.

She seemed to be concentrating on the school now. "There wouldn't be any humans in there now, right? School hasn't started for the children yet."

I settled into the bubble and squinted at her. "Why do you ask?"

Sophie shot me an impatient glare. She obviously wanted to destroy the nest, though I couldn't be sure if the building would be completely empty. There had to be someone there over summer. Did elementary kids have summer school? Janitors had to come in from time to time to keep the place clean, right? I had no idea. But the hypothetical death of even one innocent in that building made my stomach churn.

She looked back at the school and stretched both her arms toward it. All Sophie said was, "It's for the greater good," before concentrating a green ball of energy between her hands. The ball grew, her eyes flashed green, and there was nothing I could do. I remember shouting at her when she let it fly. And I remember crying a little when I saw the burst of flames and the school ablaze and crumbling. She tried to give me a tender "I understand" kind of look and touched my shoulder, but I turned away. Without another word, Sophie blasted off further skyward, rocketing away from Earth and plunging into the cosmos.

## 4: It's Dangerous to Go Alone

Our ascent into space bore an unsettling resemblance to my nightmare. Looking down at the clouds was already a familiar sort of terror from dreams in which I flew up and out of control with a speed that made me queasy. Usually, I'd fall and wake just before hitting the bottom. I admit I was a bit ashamed of myself for letting my fears get in the way of what should have been awe. I was in outer space, looking *down* at the stars, surrounded by Sophie's colorful sphere of warmth. It was as if we were cloaked by a massive, black, Swarovski-studded blanket. So many gems. Behind us, more Thruszians popped up. Behind us also lay Earth, my Earth. I'd left Earth. I was attacked by a simultaneous onslaught of nightmare flashbacks and constant reminders that I had left planet Earth and was now in outer-fucking-space. I remember Sophie asking if I was okay—I must have been hyperventilating. I saw the auburn glow of Venus in the distance. And then I was out.

*

We were still flying through space when I came to, surrounded by Thruszians and their demi-Thruszians. I kept my eyes closed to numb the shock of space-faring. I wondered how much oxygen was in this little aura bubble. Would I run out? How exactly was I supposed to get used to this? Sophie patted me on the head. "Awake now?"

"I'd like to think so," I croaked.

"Well," she said, "why don't I tell you a story to calm you down, hm?"

Part of me wanted to plead with her to take me back home. However, the other part of me didn't want to be a chicken-hearted pantywaist. So I humored her.

"All right. Go ahead."

"Remember I told you about the Earth-like planet, Naia? It was so beautiful. The first time I came to Earth, it instantly reminded me of Naia. Anyway, that was a long time ago."

It occurred to me that I had no idea how old Sophie was. "How long ago?"

"That's not important. I was sent to Naia to help investigate a possible terrorist invasion and to assist in battle. It was my first assignment, and I was terrified. God, it took so long to learn how to communicate with them. You think the 6,500 languages you Earth-humans have is a lot? Naia was run by the Aryns, the Kikopiis, and the Goraths. Their invaders, the Xenorians, outnumbered all Naians three to one and occupied a smaller planet."

"God damn."

"So you can understand why the Xenorians needed the extra space."

"So," I said, beginning to open my eyes, "you're defending the bad guys?"

"I'm just saying I understand their need. I'm not justifying the means." She sighed. "It was declared an interplanetary emergency at first. But, as the problem grew, it became an intergalactic emergency, which pulled millions of Thruszians from our assigned planets to help. I'd already been molded into the shape of a human and was preparing to make my first journey to Earth when I was drafted."

"So then what happened?"

"They took out the Kikopiis first," she said. "They were quadrupedal, catlike creatures and didn't like to stray from the Naian forests. I had the chance to get to know some of them, in one of their simple woodland civilizations. You wouldn't believe how creative they were with their tools and weapons since, you know, they didn't have thumbs."

I pictured something like ThunderCats walking on all fours.

"Their trees were taller than any you'd ever see on Earth—everything about Kikopiis was massive, their claws even." She took a moment to think. "You know, I'm pretty sure they were as big as your bears. And since I couldn't use their weapons, I had to rely solely on my own abilities, and I rode a Kikopii into battle."

"Wow." Judging from the look of utter earnestness on Sophie's face, I was sure she had no idea how badass she was making herself sound.

"His name was"—she paused—"well, I guess it wouldn't matter to you what his name was. We trampled so many Xenorians, mowed them down, but they kept coming like never-ending waves of hideous gray things. And then they brought reinforcements, this time with ships. The Kikopiis had no defense against things like that. It just wasn't... It wasn't fair." Sophie's voice cracked a little, and I heard her sniffle. "We were attacked from all directions. You could see the debris flying everywhere—splintered wood and fallen trees, heaps of soil and plant, bits and pieces of what used to be living beings. The head of a Kikopii landed in my lap, and I fell off, onto the ground. I lost my Kikopii friend somewhere in combat. God. All I saw were corpses, some smashed under fallen trees. I knew we'd lose. I guess I couldn't handle it."

"You didn't run away, did you?" I sounded like a hurt little kid, as if my favorite superhero had let the villain win.

"I did. I ran to the Aryns and Goraths because they had a better chance of survival. To this day, I still feel like scum for that."

In that moment, Sophie had never looked more human, even when she was Evangelina. Everything about her seemed softer—her face, her words. Her remorse was tangible.

"What happened with the Aryns and Goraths?" I asked.

Sophie shook her head as if coming back to her senses, ridding herself of history and memory and the emotions that tagged along. I noticed there wasn't a trace of a tear anywhere on her now.

"I'll tell you later," she said. "We're almost there."

"Almost where?"

"The Thruszian base." Sophie grinned at me. "Just look ahead."

I summoned the courage to do as she said, though slowly and with eyes initially shut. I had no idea what to expect, and I was certain anything too shocking would make my poor overworked, adrenaline-overdosed heart explode at once. I opened one eye to a slit, then the other. Already, I could see a burst of colors. Eyes fully open, I saw we were approaching a nebula—an enormous, swirling mass of ice blue, fuchsia, and jade-colored gases blossoming from a bright white center. I wasn't sure how long I'd been staring, but Sophie closed my slackened jaw for me (I realized I'd drooled a little, and I tried to be as smooth as possible about wiping it off).

"That? That's your base?"

"Our base, our birthplace."

We floated past faraway stars as if we were driving past houses and trees. I didn't remember much from the one astronomy class I took in undergrad, but I did know that we must have been traveling incomprehensibly fast. We neared the nebula in what seemed like cinematic slow motion.

"Hey, Sophie?"

"Yes?"

I cleared my throat. "So, a-about h-how fast are we, um, traveling?"

"In your units? Some 150 trillion miles per second."

My heart skipped a beat, or several. I was stuck in an awkward limbo somewhere between screaming, fainting, and just falling all to pieces. What were these Thruszians, these beings who were apparently above every law of physics? I looked at my own hands and touched my face, perhaps to see if I were any different now that I'd effectively stopped aging. I hadn't aged for some time—however long we'd been traveling. What would happen to me once I reached Earth? Would a thousand years have gone by? No, no, Sophie wouldn't let that happen. Right? I knew if I opened my mouth to ask a question, four would tumble out at once, and I was sure the answer to any one of those questions would spawn more questions and send my head whirling. I decided then that it was best to take everything involving Sophie at face value. Question nothing (which is way easier said than done).

I had to question something.

"Sophie? Am, um, am I going to be okay?"

She looked down at me. "What do you mean?"

"I mean, will I be okay when I go back to Earth? I mean. How is this possible?" I regretted it as soon as I asked.

Sophie laughed. "You'll be fine as long as you're in my care." She paused, but some look on her face suggested there was something more she wanted to say. "Technically, right now, you're imaginary."

I thought maybe I hadn't heard her correctly. "I'm sorry, what?"

"You're imaginary." When she saw that I was still confused as hell, she elaborated. "In human units, your mass is nearly 649N on Earth. Right now, your mass is an imaginary number."

I closed my eyes and shook my head. "Okay, that's enough. I'll get a headache if I even try to figure out what the hell that means."

She chuckled.

The closer we neared the nebula, the less it resembled a floral disc and began to transform before my eyes into a vast globule of color. Hundreds of Thruszians gathered and encircled the bright white nucleus with their confused and awed demi-Thruszians nestled safely in their aura spheres. Not all the Thruszians were humanoid, and those were obviously the ones not originally to Earth. So then, they mirrored the appearance of other intelligent beings elsewhere in the Milky Way: tentacled creatures, balls of light covered with large wiggling cilia, slender one-eyed slitherers. They all spoke with each other in one language, if one could call it that. It sounded to my ears like speech sped up and played backwards. Then I noticed they weren't speaking at all—communicating with each other, yes, but telepathically, which, by this time, shouldn't have surprised me. Anyway, not all of them had mouths.

Then all at once, silence. In unison, the Thruszians looked to the bright white center. I looked up at Sophie's face. Her eyes grew wide and were fixed unblinkingly on the bright white center. It was the same with the other Thruszians, the ones with eyes, anyway. What had I been dragged into? If anything happened to me out here, no one would ever know. My parents would never know. I'd never be found. What would they think of me if they were to see me as some lightning-wielding, alien-fighting freak show? What if it were my body being torn to shreds by a horde of aliens?

The Thruszians broke the silence, breathing a collective sigh. Sophie blinked a few times and appeared normal. She took a deep breath. "Well, okay then."

"What the hell was that?" That probably would have come out as a yell if my voice hadn't squeaked.

"Our Creator giving us instructions."

I ran my hands up through my hair to keep my head from falling apart. "You— You were talking to God himself?"

Sophie laughed. "No."

"Oh," I said. I saw the Thruszians starting to disperse. "So, what happens now?"

"Half of us are going to return to our assigned planets to ease the spread of the outbreak," she said. "The other half's going to try to fight this at the source."

We took off, out of the nebula and back into the vast emptiness of space.

"So, I'm going to have to go back to East Meadow?"

"Afraid so."

I was sure I'd be arrested on sight in East Meadow, and that's if they were feeling particularly generous. But I knew better than to say no to Sophie, and if I ran away, she'd find me anyway. Then again, I didn't have to let them arrest me. I had powers now, even if they were still a little hard to control. Maybe I could escape without killing anyone. My only issue was that I'd undoubtedly get shot at.

"Sophie?"

"Yes?"

"Would I die if I were shot, say, in the heart?"

She smirked hard as if trying to suppress laughter. "You're an unlocked demi-Thruszian, so you're definitely harder to kill, especially when you're powered up. But you're still human."

"So then I'd die." Nausea started to bubble up.

"Yes."

My stomach lurched, and I let out a dry heave. The second heave wasn't so dry. By the fourth, I'd propelled half my insides out into the universe.

*

After some silence, Sophie said, "Did you still want me to tell you about the Aryns and Goraths?"

"Not really." We'd been traveling for an hour and I'd stared myself into a trance, counting the stars whizzing by. It was the most I could do to retain my composure, especially since I knew once the slightest hint of Earth popped up, I'd probably lose it.

"But you were so interested before."

I looked at her. "So you guys are supposed to swoop in and save the day. Why haven't you ever interfered with something like World War II?"

Sophie huffed. "We don't bother with quarrels any smaller than something interplanetary. If the Earth-humans want to kill each other off, that's their business."

"Fair, I guess." I said, returning my gaze to the cosmos. "Well, if it eases your conscience, tell me about the Aryns or whatever."

"Bipedal aquatic mammals," Sophie gushed. "Lovely to look at, especially when they swam."

The first image that came to mind was the Majora's Mask Zoras. "Did those guys have opposable thumbs?"

"Yes." Sophie continued. "I fled that particular Kikopii forest, the one I had been living in. It didn't really make sense to me to see how any of the other Kikopiis were doing—I assumed they were all suffering the same fate. I was still quite new to all this. You know, I knew my help wouldn't have saved them, but I can't help feeling guilty for their genocide, like I'm the one to be blamed, because I left. Ethics aside, leaving to help Aryns wasn't what I was assigned to do. It was wrong all around, and it still haunts me now.

"Anyway, as I flew over one of the oceans, I came across an Aryn city. Their buildings were castle-like, elaborate and pointy, kind of like Earth's Gothic ones, and half-submerged. Their military base tried to shoot me down before realizing I was a Thruszian. They flagged me down, knowing a few of us were assigned there to help them, and I flew to them. I couldn't understand a word any of them were saying. By this time, Thruszians had been stationed all across Naia for a couple years, and these Aryns seemed a bit concerned—probably because they didn't recognize me. I wished I could tell them to send reinforcements to the Kikopiis, who were a lost cause otherwise. But I didn't know at the time that the Xenorians were on their way to the ocean at that moment. I saw Aryns and other Thruszians preparing for combat, so I joined them.

"Their guns—well, their version of guns—were hydro-powered. Appropriately so, I guess. Their ships, though, used some kind of oil-based fuel, which was what the Xenorians wanted the most, in fact. Aryns all around Naia were attacked so ruthlessly. It was ten times worse than the Kikopiis. I boarded a ship with a few others and helped man the firearms. A skyship, I mean. A few others engaged in

83

marine warfare. There was so much smoke and fire, I couldn't see anything for a while. When our ship fell under attack, we Thruszians tried to gather the remaining Aryns in our aura—like the way I'm carrying you now—but we couldn't save them all. In fact, we couldn't save very many. I'd never felt so powerless before." Sophie paused to consider something. "And since, nothing has ever made me feel more powerless than the war for Naia."

My heart sank. "I'm so sorry, Sophie."

"It's fine. They're all dead. Nothing can hurt them now."

*

When we arrived at my apartment back in East Meadow, the entire town was quiet, as it typically is, but for some reason, this didn't seem at all typical. The town was eerily still. No wind stirred the trees; most of the cars were gone. Everything was eerily still, though the rotting alien corpses built up such a stench that I dry heaved a few times—I guessed I'd barfed out all I had out in space. I wondered where all the FBI agents had gone. It was as if that crowd of people had never been there. Sophie and I exchanged glances.

"First thing," she said, "we have to clean up this mess. I don't think there are any more viruses here, so we can go to wherever else has an infestation."

"But we're staying on Earth, right?"

"Yes, we're staying on Earth."

"Good." I looked around at the dead aliens and damaged vehicles and wondered if my parents were all right. If they'd seen footage of me, maybe they would have called. "Where are we going after this, do you know?"

Sophie had aimed her arms at a pile of cadavers and was burning them with light beams. "No idea. Wherever we're needed, I guess."

"So," I said, "does that mean I can check my phone? Maybe after this, we could stop by my hometown."

When she stopped her steady stream of matter-pulverizing light, all that remained of the pile were ashes and crumbs. "Sure, though there's always the possibility that a Thruszian might already be there taking care of it, in which case we couldn't stay long."

"I understand."

She gave me a wary look before starting to burn the next pile. That look said what she knew I'd rather not hear. *Or, your parents could already be gone.* I looked up at my busted apartment window.

"My parents are going to freak when they find out about this wreck." My failed attempt at lightening things up.

"It is a rather nice place. Why'd they shack you up here instead of somewhere closer to campus?"

I shrugged. "They didn't want me going too far from them, or something like that. They weren't very happy when I chose Skylight Heights because it was so far, but it's got pretty much the best electrical engineering program in the country, and I was top of my class. So, compromise—I can live all the way out here if I stay in a 'safe environment.'"

"Fair enough, though little did they know," Sophie said. "Go get your phone, then come back and help me out."

As I walked up the staircase, it occurred to me that I didn't have my keys, which didn't bother me much. As this point, Sophie could just fly me up. There was no more damage to be done. East Meadow had forever lost its pristine reputation for normality, and somehow that made me want to smile. When I got there, my apartment door was ajar, and the lock was broken. I didn't have to open the door all the way to assess the damage. My La-Z-Boy had been flipped over. I saw a drawer on its side, contents spilled and scattered. I hesitated to open the door the rest of the way, fearing there would be someone inside. But why would anyone be in there now? For all I knew, the town seemed evacuated. But then again, East Meadow wasn't normal anymore. Anything could be in there. I braced myself and pushed the door open.

Someone on the other side swung it the rest of the way open for me. My first instinct was to power up and shoot, but it was only a slight girl about my age. She looked harmless. Pissed, but harmless. I powered down.

The girl looked me up and down and sneered. "I really hoped it wouldn't come to this."

I blinked. "I'm sorry, who are you?" I pushed past her into my apartment. "And what—what did you do? And why?"

My first mistake was assuming she was harmless. As I looked around and assessed the damage, something fast and hard struck the back of my head. I fell to the floor with a terrible headache. Before I could whirl around and confront the crazy bitch, I saw her foot fly at my face. I rolled to dodge.

"Seriously, what the fuck?" I exclaimed, jumping to my feet. She started toward me again, and I held out a hand to stop her. She was a small girl, and I really didn't want to hurt her.

"I know what you are," she said.

"Oh? What's that? A guy, a grad student, Asian, the list goes on."

The girl's eyes narrowed to little slits. It made her look a little scary. "No, a demi."

That sobered me pretty quickly. "What?"

"You know, I bet your parents were lovely, normal people," she said, crossing her arms. "And I'm sure they lived nice, normal lives before you came along. I know because I'm a demi, too."

I rubbed my temples, trying to understand what she was talking about. "First of all, what do you know about my parents? Second of all, why are you here?"

"Idiot." She rolled her eyes. "They probably did the same thing my parents did, sent you to East Meadow for help because they knew there was something different about you. And East Meadow is pretty much Normal, U.S.A."

"Okay?" I shrugged. "What does what your parents did to you have to do with me?"

The girl sighed and paced the floor. "You know Mrs. Baxter."

"Yes. So?"

She stopped and looked me dead in the eye. "That's my grandmother. I was sent to live with her to even me out."

"Sucks to suck," I said.

"Well, joke's on you. I turned out just fine," she spat, lunging at me again. I ducked and rolled, so close to powering up. "Obviously you were a lost cause," she said. "But you know this whole demi business is wrong, right? It's not natural. We're mutations.

And I'm not going to stand by and let the likes of us ruin the integrity of the natural order. And I'm certainly not going to fight for your silly cause."

"Whoa, whoa," I said. "That 'silly cause' you're talking about is *saving our planet*."

She scoffed and began pacing again. "Oh really? Is that what your Thruszian told you, too? Do you even know what they are? How do you know they're not plotting an invasion?"

"Well, look, girly," I said. "You're you. If you want to make up conspiracy theories and hate yourself, that's your business."

Then a thought occurred to me. "Wait... Was... Was Mrs. Baxter in on this?"

"No!" She snapped. The entire apartment shook, knocking me back. I then realized, to my lasting horror, that this crazy demi had powers over earth.

"My grandmother showed me nothing but kindness. She would have done the same for you, had you appreciated her more. She never knew what I was. She never knew I had powers. I was a good, church-going girl! I may be an abomination," she cried, "but at least I struggle against it. I bet you flaunt your talents like the shameless heathen you are."

"What, this?" I sparked up one hand. "Look, if you want me out of this town, I was already leaving, so..."

The girl shook her head. "That's not enough. I didn't spend months tracking down every single demi in the surrounding area to just let one run free now."

"So what are you going to do to me now? Kill me?"

Without another word, the crazy girl leaped at me, wrapped her hands around my neck, and squeezed. I bent over and lurched, hurling her over my shoulder into the wall. As I held my own throat and gasped for air, the girl lay crumpled before me. She shuddered a little, groaned, and rose to her feet.

"You don't know what you're fighting for," she said, flushed and indignant, hair strewn over her face like a psycho from the movies.

Sophie called for me from outside, but before I could react, this girl threw herself at me again, this time propelling us out the busted window.

5: For Those About to Rock

I powered up on impulse—thank god for subconscious reflexes—so I wasn't hurt when we fell. The girl didn't appear hurt, either. I kicked her off and rolled over to Sophie.

"So-phie," I said between huffs, "You... know... this crazy ass... carrot top?"

"I'm not a carrot top!" The pavement under me shook and rose like a platform. "I'm a strawberry blonde. And my name's Katie."

I leaped from the heap of rock before it could crush me. Sophie ran to my side. "I actually think I know her Thruszian."

"Oh my god," I cried. "You knew Mrs. Baxter was harboring a small psycho?"

Sophie blinked. "Missus who?"

Katie charged up and lifted more hunks of earth. I grabbed Sophie's arm. "I'll explain later." We dodged both of Katie's flying boulders and hid behind a truck. "And when we get through this, you can please explain where the hell her Thruszian is?"

The truck rose and was thrown down the street. Katie approached us, arms quaking with energy. "I killed him."

"Liar!" I jumped up. "You can't kill Thruszians."

"Actually," Sophie chimed in, "you can damage their physical body so much that it disappears..." She stood slowly, addressing Katie. "Was Ythril Zetyld supposed to be taking care of you? Did you really kill his human body?"

Katie crossed her arms. Attacking me was one thing. She was smart enough to know there was absolutely nothing she could do against Sophie in her Thruszian form. "Why do you care? Siblings or something?"

"We're all siblings," Sophie replied. I wondered then if "Zetyld" was the name of their Creator, if it had a name.

Katie's blue eyes flicked between us. She was a pretty girl—pink cheeks, red lips, and all. It was a shame she was so hell-bent on killing me. "So, if he's not really dead," she asked, "is he going to come after me?"

"Not for a long time. It takes ages to regenerate after something like that," Sophie said, serenely as usual, though I could sense an inkling of sorrow in her words. "But why did you do it?"

Katie clenched her fists, and various metal poles and patches of sidewalk shook and crumbled. "Because I can't... He wanted me to... It's wrong!"

Sophie frowned. "What's wrong? Saving the planet?"

"Stop calling it that! It's unnatural!" Katie whimpered. "I'm unnatural. And I know you aliens are all lying to us. So, if I'm going to be cursed like this, I may as well use it to help get rid of abominations like us."

I watched her body quiver and her face grow red, fighting tears. "You do realize why we're here, right?" I said. "There's evidence all around us that Earth's being attacked by some virus, and we have to save it. We're the only ones who can, actually." It all sounded so ludicrous spoken out loud. My life had effectively turned into a comic book.

Katie huffed. "Well, if it's a natural end, then so be it."

I powered down in hopes that she'd follow suit and regain composure. After some hesitation, she let her arms fall limp and her head drop, and the ambient quaking ceased. Sophie and I exchanged glances but said nothing. She seemed just as lost for words as I was.

"Oh, opal." Katie's voice was faint. She sniveled and stooped to pick up a chunk of rock embedded with something pale and shiny. "What are the odds?"

Sophie went to examine one of the holes Katie had made in her kill-River rampage. After peering down for a while, Sophie plummeted headfirst. She soon resurfaced. "You don't want to fall down this hole, though it could make you a lot of money."

Katie turned the opal over in her palm. "It's one of my favorites."

"How did you know what it was?" I asked.

"They say it's impossible," she said, "but I can tell what rocks and gems are just by looking at them and touching them and stuff. That's why I wanted to major in physical geology, to use my gift to maybe help people somehow, but that would have been unfair. I wouldn't really have to work for it."

Her words hit me like stone. I examined my own hands, astonished. I made them spark, felt the energy of what was left of the power lines coursing through my veins. That must have been what Katie meant by shamelessly flaunting my ability. This both elated and saddened me—so I wasn't some kind of wonder kid with a natural understanding of electricity and herculean quantities of math. I was just an unlocked demi-Thruszian. Without these powers, I probably would have been a nobody. I'd probably still be an undergrad. Suddenly, none of my academic accomplishments seemed real anymore. Maybe Katie was right. Maybe it was unfair.

Sophie approached us now. "Ythril won't be coming back for a while, but I can take you both under my wing." When she tried to place her hand on Katie's shoulder, the girl whipped around and threw Sophie's hand off.

"No! It's wrong."

"So is destroying your town to kill one person," I mumbled.

They both ignored me. Sophie continued. "Do you know what the virus is, Katie?"

Katie clenched her fists again. The street trembled. "Obviously it was something that was supposed to happen. Leave me alone." She threw a punch, sending a wave of pavement hurtling toward me. Sophie jumped in to save me, and in the meantime, Katie ran off.

*

Sophie and I sat in the ruins of the elementary school after I'd begged her to help me make sure there were no human remains. We'd found none. I sat on a huge chunk of cement, exhausted. She sat near me because there was nothing else for her to do. I could tell she wanted to get going, but she was generous enough to allow me my moment, which, I was sure, was just another human thing she didn't fully understand, regardless of whether or not she claimed to. Sophie sucked in a long drag of air and lay back on the rubble.

"You know," she said, "I really don't understand demis like Katie."

"I don't understand humans like Katie."

"Thankfully, we outnumber nutcases like her." After some time of silence, Sophie stood and started powering up to fly. "But come on. We can't waste any more time here. Are we off to your parents'?"

I stood reluctantly, taking one last look around at what used to be a school for children. There weren't very many, but their yelps and squawks could carry and seemed to gain additional momentum while I was studying at my desk. But I suppose I didn't always mind them. A handful of kindergarteners had performed a rather charming, badly coordinated little dance at Mrs. Crabapple's wedding reception. I chuckled at it now. That caught Sophie's attention, and she asked what was so funny.

I snickered. "Just little kid dances."

Sophie nodded, though her face betrayed that she didn't understand. "Right."

I held on to her, and we soared off. She shouted over the wind, "I never did understand the whole dancing phenomenon. Singing, maybe. But even that is, well, strange."

"What do you mean strange?" I had to squint to see and hesitated to open my mouth too much so as not to choke on any bugs.

"Have you ever thought about it?" she replied. "Singing and dancing have functions in other species—mating and alerting others to danger and things like that—but what do humans do it for? It's so bizarre."

"So Thruszians don't sing or dance?"

"Never." She paused to consider something, then said, "I mean, some of us have tried, in an effort to understand. I tried dancing once, for a whole semester."

"Oh," I said. "Oh." What was Sophie Zetyld? Definitely not of Earth, not human, and after reaching our presumed victory—at least, after Earth is eradicated—I assumed she'd leave, forever. For reasons I couldn't yet articulate, that disheartened me. She did say once that she wanted to retire, whatever that meant for her, and live on Earth. Pipe dreams of a celestial being.

I gave the surface below a few cursory glances. East Meadow resembled a ghost town. Its absolute stillness was unsettling to me, and I gathered that it was because the entire suburb looked as if it froze in the middle of the day's routine and everybody was suddenly abducted. While most cars were gone, a few still sat in driveways, waiting for the commute to work the next morning. Fresh, green lawns stretched out before clean houses. Dust collected on nothing; smatterings of nature remained in neat little patches designated by town admins. It chilled me. And then we ascended further into the sky until I could see East Meadow no more.

Sophie flew me the 350 miles to my parents' home in about ten minutes, far above the clouds, enclosing us in her aura bubble when the air became too cold and thin for me. I couldn't see any of the goings-on below and wondered if we'd passed any alien-infested towns on the way to my parents'. I hoped not. I knew it must have taken a lot of restraint for Sophie to pass these vast patches of Earth without checking for signs of invasion, just so I could see my parents and let them know I was all right.

When we were close to landing in Liandra, the suburb where I grew up, I looked up at Sophie's face. It seemed hard somehow—focused, troubled, worried. I grabbed her hand, and when she looked at me, her face softened. The neighborhood hadn't changed since I moved to East Meadow. We passed my parents' church, the tiny shopping plaza that had my favorite bagel place, my high school, the flower garden of Liandra Commons. Seeing the familiar landmarks again and knowing that it might all be destroyed set off a sharp twinge of pain in my stomach. On the bright side, though, the town looked untouched by the virus. Sophie brought us to a soft landing about half a block away from my childhood home.

"I'm going to take a look around the area," she said, though she wasn't looking at me. Her eyes darted everywhere, and it made me nervous.

"What is it?" I asked. "Do you sense something?"

She gave me that weak smile again. "No, I'm just being alert." She nodded ahead. "You go visit your parents. I'll be back soon."

I meant to ask how soon, but she took off. Left alone, I took a deep breath and walked ahead, passing cars, houses, and even lawns that hadn't changed since I was small. My parents' house is a golden-brown colonial with tan accents, its paint regularly renewed. The lawn is large and neat, ringed by my mother's flower garden. The phlox fragrance was heavenly. I climbed the stairs to the door and rang the bell. Even though all the evidence strongly suggested that my parents were likely all right, waiting was still agonizing. The lock clicked on the other side, and I exhaled, relieved.

The door opened to my father's startled face—eyes widened and eyebrows through the roof. I dove in for a bear hug, and he stiffened. My dad is not exactly a fan of hugging, but he tolerates it from me, sometimes.

"You're in town," he said, still startled.

"I am!" I said. "I just wanted to surprise you and said hi."

He patted my back, which had the double meaning of *I'm glad to see you* and *Get off me*. When I let him free, he turned away from the door and called to my mother, who came rushing over from the living room. I'd never been happier to see them. I fought back tears as my mother welcomed me in and complained that I didn't call first so she could cook something for me. I removed my shoes at the door and took a good look at the living room—its spare mint walls and white Victorian furniture. Sunlight shone through the sheer curtains of the living room's many windows. And though the house was immaculate, she told me to excuse the "mess," and that had I called ahead of time, she would have had the house looking better.

"Papa and I miss you. You never call," she said, ushering me to the couch. "Sit. I'll make you something. You don't look like you're eating."

"Mom, I've been eating."

"Eating what, grass?"

My dad cleared his throat and sat in the chair across from me. He was never quite as expressive as my mother, but it was nice to see his quiet smile.

"Well?" He looked at me expectantly. "How are classes?"

"They haven't started yet."

"Where are you staying?" Mom asked. "Not a hotel, I hope. I'll fix up your room. Where are your bags? Also, did you find a church?"

As my mother looked around the room for my non-existent luggage, I struggled with how I should explain my visit.

"I'm, um... I'm actually not staying that long."

My parents stared at me as if I'd just told them I was dropping out of school.

"I'm just in town for today," I continued. "And I really can't stay long. I just, um... I just wanted to stop in and make sure you guys were all right."

Mom and Dad exchanged glances. Then my dad said, "There's something wrong."

"You're in trouble." Mom joined me on the couch.

I sighed. How could I explain that I was out to save the world to my innocent parents? Neither spent much time on the Internet, so I wondered if they even knew about the alien virus.

"I'm not really the one that's in trouble, per se," I said. "Um. Has anything weird been on the news lately, that you've seen? Like, weird creatures, ugly green things, um... comets?"

I'd expected them to give me weird looks, but there was something profoundly knowing in their faces. Each betrayed a flash of recognition when I mentioned comets. My eyes flickered between them as they exchanged glances again. Now, my heart was pounding.

Mom placed a light hand on my knee. "We shouldn't have let you go so far away."

"What do you mean?"

"When you were a child you would"—she paused to think of the word—"spark."

My heart stopped. "Spark?"

Dad chimed in. "Like little lightning. We were too embarrassed to tell anyone, so we handled by ourselves."

"That is why," Mom said, "we didn't want you to move so far away."

"Wait a minute, wait a minute." I stood. "You knew I was like this?"

Mom looked down at her lap and didn't say anything for a while. "There was a shooting star. You were two years old. I opened the window and held you up so you could see."

"What?" I said. "What happened?"

"The star came toward us! I scream and shut the blinds, and you cried, and after that, you started to spark," she said, eyes still downcast. "We had to teach you sparking was bad. Sometimes our lights went out!"

I was speechless.

"We worried about what would happen if you went far away," Dad said. "Lucky we knew Mrs. Valentine and Mrs. Baxter. We thought East Meadow would be good for you."

"Yes," Mom nodded. "Nothing happens in East Meadow, so nothing to trigger you."

I felt weak and needed to lean against the wall for balance. "But, you knew, and you never told me?"

"We didn't really know what you were." Mom looked at me now. "We still don't know what you are."

I took deep breaths and counted to ten. There was so much to explain. At the same time, there was still so much I needed to understand. One month ago, I found out I was part-Thruszian and that aliens exist. And that Earth was in trouble. And that the comet I'd been watching was actually my Thruszian. My academic abilities weren't truly my own. My parents kept this enormous secret from me. And now I had to run off and save the world.

I laughed mirthlessly. "Brilliant. This is brilliant."

A quick glance out the window informed me that Sophie was flying toward us. Part of me wanted to curl up in a corner and wait for the world to come crashing down around me. I hadn't asked for any of this. But then, neither had my parents. Neither had Sophie, really. The penitent looks on my parents' faces broke my heart. I couldn't leave them like this.

I stood up straight and resolved to leave them with something at least a little positive. "I know what I am. I'm a demi-Thruszian, and I know you don't know what that means, but it's a good thing. I'm basically a protector of Earth. You protected me; now, I get to return the favor."

No one said anything until there was a knock on the window. I looked through the curtains, and there was Sophie. Her face was urgent. I nodded at her and made a mental note to thank her for not bursting in and giving my parents a heart attack.

"Who was knocking on the window?" Mom craned her neck to see.

I blocked the window with my body. "I'll explain later. I'll come back as soon as I can!"

As I hurried to open the door and bolt out, I could see my parents in the corner of my eye standing and trying to see who was at the window. Sophie tried to say something to me, but I grabbed her wrist and ran as quickly as I could out of view from any of the living room windows. We ended up at the side of the house, and I let her go.

"Sorry about that," I huffed. "But you'd give my parents a heart attack."

Sophie waved dismissively. "We've got bigger problems."

"Yeah?" I felt a raindrop on my nose. Then two on my hand. Behind Sophie, dark clouds were rolling in. "Don't tell me we've got a nest around here."

"I wish that was all," she said. "Come on. I'll explain on the way."

She grabbed me, and up we flew, to my dismay, toward the oncoming storm.

Sophie continued. "There's a young one 50 miles from here. The real problem is the horde festering about 180 miles away."

"A horde?" I said. "You mean like the attack that happened in East Meadow?"

"No. This is far bigger than that."

I was afraid of the answer, but I had to ask. "How much bigger?"

Sophie glanced at me over her shoulder. "There are already Thruszians and demis there fighting, and it's not looking good."

## 6: This is the War Room

A faint rumble of thunder rolled in with the clouds, and Sophie and I sailed through the growing mist. As the mist evolved into drizzle, and the drizzle into showers, Sophie enveloped us in her aura bubble, and we continued to fly in silence out of Liandra and over the highways. Flashes of lightning, initially distant and small, made my body tingle. It only intensified as we flew further into the storm. Every time lightning struck, I felt a lurch in my core. The closer the lightning bolt, the stronger the jerk in the pit of my stomach and the flash of energy through my veins. I felt Sophie pat me tenderly on the head, her warm, staticky thumb brushing against the nape of my neck. I thought I was going to melt through the aura sphere.

"I can't take this storm," I said.

"You'll harness it," Sophie said. "Power up. It'll help."

I was petrified by flashbacks of my nightmare. I could still feel Venus' lightning striking through me. Everything bolted in and out of my mind: the nightmare, my fake talents, my parents' faces. In this moment, I couldn't help thinking that even though I knew *what* I was, as I'd told my parents, I had no idea *who* I was anymore. It all came down to an accident, a coincidence in spacetime, and here was this tormenting lightning rubbing it all in my face. Making me its bitch. My gut convulsed.

"Did you hear me?" Sophie said. "Power up."

"Are you sure that won't make it worse?" But, again, I should have known better than to question Sophie. Pushing through the pain, I powered up and let the lightning sustain me. To my surprise, it didn't feel like complete death. In fact, if you forgive the cliché, I'd never felt more alive. Sophie asked how I felt, to which I replied with maniacal laughter. I was drunk with power. My thirst for the aliens' precious bodily fluids was palpable.

Sophie made a face. "Can you at least contain yourself until we get to the next battleground?"

"Okay." I wrapped my arms around myself in a feeble attempt to pacify my irresistible, lightning-induced urge to pulverize. I needed a distraction. "You never told me about the Goraths."

"Oh," she said. "Right." Sophie took in a deep breath and began. "Well, I actually did stay with the Aryns until the very end. Before they were completely wiped out, they were savvy enough to call in reinforcements from the remaining Kikopiis and Goraths. By that time, the Kikopii race was basically extinct. Now, the Goraths were the closest to what humans are like, I guess—humanoid, bipedal, fleshy with patches of hair, but they were gargantuan compared your puny species."

"Thanks."

Sophie paused to think, as if recalling something fond. She seemed less stressed, and I like to think I helped her regain her composure by talking about Naia.

She said, "They were all shades of red and orange, some yellow, so when they poured in in waves, it was like fire sweeping across the ocean and sky. They broke through the smoke and debris, charging like Asgardians in Ragnarök." At this reference, Sophie smiled sadly. "But we all know how Ragnarök ends."

I squeezed myself, sobering up from my intoxication with power. "But you don't think Earth will meet the same fate. Do you?"

Sophie glanced at me, then back down at the flooding roads below. "Who's to tell? But I'm not running away this time. I may not have known the Goraths long, but when they were all that was left…" Her voice trailed off and her eyes sharpened.

"What else happened with the Goraths?" I pressed. My muscles jerked. I needed to stay distracted—the jitters were returning.

"No time." Sophie made a death drop to the ground, toward a horde of aliens terrifying citizens in their cars. Further down the highway, the horde swelled far as I could see, consuming the boundless traffic jam. Combating them were other Thruszians and demis, along with the odd patches of police or military forces. My heart walloped in my chest. The urge was overwhelming.

"Throw me down!" I shouted.

Sophie released me from her orb, and I dove down to join the great fight, eager to spill blood, rip limbs, and spark up.

I crash-landed with a white flash on the roof of someone's car, which was covered in blood and half-chewed through by the aliens. Sparks and bolts shot out around me like starbursts; bodies, both human and nonhuman, flew; the earth faltered and cracked in places; and above me, Sophie emitted a blast of starlight and emerged as a horse—a unicorn(!)—colossal and dazzling as if a constellation had come to life. And off she rode into glory, blasting aliens by the dozens. Deadly rainbow beams erupted from the tip of her alicorn.

A demi slammed into the side of the car as if badly hit but jumped back up, blades of light on his arms twinkling through the rain. He severed the heads of every alien in an eight-foot radius in one spiraling sweep. When he looked up at me, he sort of reminded me of Jensen Case. A goofy-looking kid.

"Welcome to the party!" he shouted.

I jumped down next to him and beefed up my powers. "River."

"Rob."

We nodded at each other and sprinted off into the chaos together. I shot streams of thunder down the streets, between cars, wrecking scores of aliens. Rob and I covered each other's backs, almost as synchronized as the choreographed fights in action films—it was unreal. Not far away, a demi harnessed the rain around her to wash away oncoming hordes charging toward the highway.

"Where did they all come from?" I shouted.

"Hell if I know," Rob shouted back. "But they ain't dying fast enough."

Above, the Thruszians all looked like nebular gods. Below, I wish I could be so pretentious as to say we were like X-men. I sure felt that way. Thunder boomed close

93

by, and a wave of static energy surged through me. And I knew. I yelled for Rob to stand far back, and then it came—a bolt of lightning shot straight through me. I channeled it, and the rest of the fight was a fast-forward series of light and color that would put XTC to shame. Flash! Foot. Guts. Blue. Fist. Face. Whirl. Green. Duck. Kick. Leap. Fist. Fist. Fist. Red. Flash! Further down the highway, officers helped citizens escape from their vehicles and evacuate to safety. Wet. Slip. Flash! Burn. Bright. Red. Duck. Swoosh. Green. Fist. Kick. Fist. Another demi—a hulking woman—picked up the empty cars and hurled them at aliens coagulating in open field space. Whirl. Kick. Foot. Face. Face. Face. Great balls of fire plummeted from the Thruszians above, toward the aliens further out in the fields. There seemed to be no end. At one point I stumbled over something and saw that it was the body of a demi, lacerated beyond recognition. Somewhere, a crowd of aliens ambushed and swallowed a demi, who would have died had her Thruszian not come and pulled her—limp and bleeding— from the horde. Katie glimmered in the back of my mind. Flash! Flash! Flash! Flash!

I didn't have time to process these fragments of thought. Green creatures, larger than normal, leapt from car tops. Many landed on me, repeatedly. I fried them as they came, but I could feel myself fading. They piled faster than I could fend them off. The first teeth clamped down on my shoulder, like being stabbed by twenty little knives. I was sure no one heard me scream. Through a gap in my slimy cage, I saw some of them feeding on someone's family dog and growing in size. Then, I could see nothing.

I was sure I'd met my doom when duel slivers of beamlike blades slashed through the cage of aliens. I couldn't see well but could tell it was Rob. He dropped to his knees and held me up; my head lolled.

"You're blinking out, man!"

What? I mustered the energy to raise my arm, which was flickering like a dying bulb. "Blinking..."

"Yes, blinking out! We've got to..." His words trailed off. I could see his lips moving though there was no sound—no sound other than the muted crashes of faraway fireballs. The earth shook, and I caught glimpses of the contorted, screamless mouths of demis, raging green bodies thrashing flesh and steel alike, Thruszians dropping from the sky like meteorites to save their demis. Above me, I saw Sophie transform back to normal, and for a moment, I thought she was going to fly down to save me. She seemed so far away, and she tilted her head as if I were a lost cause...

Bright! Glow.

Sophie's warm, lavender face blocked everything else from sight. Her eyes were tense, and her mouth moved as if saying something severe. When I didn't respond, she shook me and tried again. I heard her say my name, and she held me close. Muffled words: "... okay... one last... spacetime... might... exist... please... die... this anymore..." Then she was gone.

Bright. Brighter. *Brilliant.* Hot. White hot. The world dissolved into twilight.

*

At that time, I thought that I and the world as I knew it had ceased to exist. But here I am, a week later, nursing my subsiding aches. I start co-op soon. I sit in my La-Z-Boy, surveying my living room, in which everything is left as it was before the first "comet" spotting. In fact, my telescope is still in my closet, collecting dust. I feel cheated, a victim of a cheap story ending. All that time and memory wasted. And then there were the first couple days of wondering whether or not I was losing my mind.

There is something different about East Meadow now. I don't think the Bartletts even *exist* anymore—at least, they never lived *here*. I've seen new faces that have been here longer than I've been born. But the biggest difference is that I finally feel like I can breathe. Mrs. Baxter and Mrs. Valentine—sporting fresh, youthful haircuts from some Skylight salon—wave to me as I start up my car and head to campus.

Skylight University is the same. I read another text from my mom asking about church. While still in the comfort and privacy of my driver's seat, I want so badly to see if I can still spark up, but the idea of it makes me nauseous. Some other time, then. The parking garage is full of cars, one of which I know I saw on the highway during the battle. Is Rob still around? Does he live in Liandra? And then I try to remember what Sophie was trying to say to me right before everything ended. *Last, spacetime, die,* and *anymore* are all I can remember, and I can't help but feel something slightly ominous about that. I wonder if she got her wish.

Walking down the crowded hallways, I think I see Katie ambling out of a physical geology lab, but her face is slightly different—though, I can't place my finger on how. But that lustrous, orange-kissed hair is definitely the same.

Most of my friends are still here, and I finish out the week trying to catch Katie or even Jensen Case in my periphery. I know better than to look for Evangelina (but I still try). The alien virus can no longer be found anywhere on the Internet. I know, because I spent an embarrassing sum of hours searching even the most obscure crannies of the World Wide Web. I'm actually searching in a café now, venti espresso in my trembling hand, when a tap on my shoulder nearly sends me rocketing out of my seat. Someone asks if this seat is free—most of the others are taken. I shrug. It's a free country. The first thing I notice is the familiar cascade of curling braids. I close my laptop, close my eyes, and try to will her away.

"You're not real."

Evangelina sighs. "Do we have to have this conversation again?"

"I'm obviously comatose."

"No, you're not comatose." Her tone suggests there is more. I open my eyes. "You're definitely alive and well, grasshopper."

All I can do is stare.

"Aren't you going to ask me a million questions now?"

I shake my head. "What's the point? I could be dead, I could be comatose, this could be a parallel universe or a different dimension, and if any of those things were true, you wouldn't tell me. Or if you did, I wouldn't believe you. Or if I believed you, what's the point?" I fix my eyes on my coffee. "I'm stuck here, wherever here is."

Evangelina laughs. "You're learning."

I manage a smile. She mirrors me. In this version of reality, she's as likely as not my ticket to the looney bin. I'm not sure if she's human or Thruszian, but she sure devours a veggie pie without issue. I'd never seen her eat before. She wipes a speck of sauce from the corner of her mouth and giggles, a faint blush growing on dark skin, just barely tinting her nose and cheeks.

# Evangelina's Dream

### I. Negatio

I'm not quite sure I will ever understand the bizarre phenomenon that is dreaming, no matter how long I reside in this humanoid state. River lies beside me now, snoring softly like a kitten. I brush his bangs lightly, and he stirs, though doesn't wake. He doesn't know that somewhere, in a parallel universe, his original universe, he is dead. I salvaged his consciousness to bring him with me here, to this version of Earth. I don't think I will ever tell him. I insist that all of his powers are gone and hint that I am only human, that Sophie is gone forever. These are lies. But the longer I stay human, the more profoundly I can dream and feel emotion. Eating is still a challenge, though a vegan diet seems to sit well for now. I run a hand along his bare shoulder, flesh against flesh. It still makes me quiver. More and more, I am learning that Earthling bodies are fine-tuned machines, simultaneously strong and delicate, and after getting past the fact that humans are essentially meat-machines full of water, I can begin to see their bodies as beautiful, intricate things. River sometimes catches me examining my reflection in the bathroom mirror. Some nights, I stand naked in front of his door mirror, and River hugs me from behind and kisses my neck. It is sensations like these—so deliciously human!—that keep me going. And it is things like dreams that keep me wondering.

His phone says it's 6:04 a.m., two hours before sunrise. I'm not sure I'm going to get back to sleep before the alarm goes off, not after that extraordinarily clairvoyant dream I just had.

My first memory of the dream started in a long-gone forest of Naia. Lush greenery and gargantuan trees expanded for countless miles in all directions, studded with bright, neon flowers and vines. Not far away, wooden domes the size of huts sat undisturbed, perched in the treetops or nestled in the ground. This was where a population of Kikopiis used to dwell before the whole species was wiped out. Remembering this, remembering the war, I knew something wasn't right. I smelled smoke. If I flew fast enough, I could beat the flames, but I could not fly. I wasn't Sophie. I was powerless Angie. And so, I did all that I could think to do—kicked the ground and cursed. This was not the death I was supposed to have.

The smoke swelled and the flames flourished around me. Coughing and rubbing my stinging eyes, I dropped to my knees and waited, hoping I'd suffocate to death before the fire engulfed my little spot in the woods. My own name echoed between my ears as I crouched. But why? Why wasn't my life flashing before my eyes? Why just my name? Then, it grew louder.

"Soffialexinus!"

I clamped my hands over my ears as if that would help, and burrowed my forehead into the soil, trying to will this voice away. It sounded too much like Ythril, a

96

fellow Thruszian, also assigned to Earth. My best friend, my brother. But it couldn't be him. Right about now, he'd be regenerating back at the home base, in the warmth and safety of our birth nebula. He would not be free for some time.

A hand grabbed my shoulder and I jumped. When I looked up, squinting through smoke and stinging tears, I could barely make out Ythril's face peering down at me. This was undoubtedly an illusion, another side effect of being human.

Ythril reached for my hand. "Sophie, come on!"

I decided I preferred this hallucination to watching my life flash before my eyes, and I grabbed his hand.

"You can make this," he said, cradling me in his lavender arms. "Come on."

There are billions of Thruszians across the omniverse, so it's easy for many to drop off the radar of one's memory. And we don't always get along. But the first time I spotted Ythril, all lavender with a blue-green alicorn like mine, I never forgot him.

I wanted to tell him I really wasn't going to make it, but all that came out of my mouth were coughs. I wanted to say he knew as well as I that smoke is highly toxic to humans. You see, Thruszians don't "breathe," as such. He flew me out of the forest, toward the sky, assuring me I'd be okay. But I knew what would happen. Ythril held me close as he picked up speed, shooting toward outer space like a rocket.

*Wait*, I wanted to say, *I'll burn.*

"Not much longer now!" He shouted.

The air thinned, and I was freezing.

*Ythril, stop! I'll burn, and I'll feel it!*

This hallucination, this cruel trick of Evangelina's mind, treated me as if I were in Thruszian form.

"Here we go!"

"I'll burn!" I screamed. As he propelled us toward the stars, I shut my eyes and braced myself. And then, I heard nothing.

When I finally opened my eyes and looked around, Ythril was nowhere to be seen, though without him, I continued to fly through the vast, dark emptiness of space. There was no hope of slowing down or stopping, and I watched helplessly as the beautiful, burning planet of Naia faded from my sight.

After 67 failed attempts at trying to transform back into a Thruszian, it occurred to me that all of the gases should have been ripped from my body by the vacuum. All my saliva should have boiled away, and yet I spat in one direction and watched it fly. *So then*, I thought, *this is still part of the hallucination. Is this really what people experience when they are dying?* I waited. It seemed as if hours of nothingness passed me by. I began to realize that something was off, but, as often happens in dreams, I could not quite figure out what.

After some time, a soft wave of heat kissed my back. I turned myself around and beheld a glowing ball the size of, maybe, a meteorite. It was perfectly spherical and looked like a miniature neutron star. Curious, I swam toward it, and then suddenly, when I was close to it, it sucked me in.

II. Iracundia

Down, down I fell, away from the external brightness, into a pitch blackness for some time. I thought maybe I was being punished for something, but what had I done? Had I been Evangelina for too long? I can't say I don't miss my Thruszian form—flawless, unyielding, ranging the colors of a galaxy. River likes to call it "kaleidoscopic." I thought of him as I plummeted further into oblivion: how he spent a month making sure I knew proper Korean manners for when I meet his parents, even though I wanted to tell him that I'm billions of years old and have been everywhere on Earth at least a hundred times; how every time he manages to slip up in the eyes of East Meadow, half the time, he gets away by blaming Victor Cho; how he pretended not to have received any of Victor's emails asking him to please stop framing him. Thinking about these things, I laughed despite myself.

The hole down which I fell took on a soft, red glow, and I felt intense bursts of heat pumping up from somewhere below. When I looked down, I could see what looked like a viscous pool of lava, and my heart jumped. Where the hell was I? I didn't quite land. I mean, there was no precise end to my fall. I just sort of appeared on a glass floor, under which lava flowed with the speed of a tortoise. Around me, the walls were made of deep red rock, and there was a small, round doorway. It was my only exit, as the walls were too smooth to climb, but I hesitated. My braids were hot and heavy against my neck, so I tied them up, remembering, with some irritation, that human bodies sweat. Wiping my damp neck, I approached the little doorway, under which I had to duck. It led to a similar room, but bigger, and with caged chambers built into the walls. In one directly opposite, I immediately recognized Ythril and ran to him. He brightened when he saw me, pressing himself against the bars.

"Sophie!"

"Ythril! What," I said, "*What* are you doing here? What is this place? Why are you locked up like a prisoner?"

"I think it's perfectly comfortable here."

"You think it's *what*?"

Ythril motioned for me to come in. "It's really quite comfortable. Here, let me open the door..."

"You're not locked in here?" I asked, hopelessly confused.

"No, not really," he said, "but I'm visiting someone who is. You might remember her."

"What? Who?"

A flame-colored Thruszian with a sour face sauntered into the dim light from the shadows. She had no hair and two small, scarlet antlers instead of an alicorn. It took me a moment to remember.

"Lieneux?" I said. Lieneux had also been assigned to Earth. "What happened?"

Lieneux crossed her arms. "What do you think happened? Caught space-hopping. Again."

I stared at her in horror. I myself had space-hopped when I was desperate to find the existence of Naia in a parallel universe. After that failed, I did it again when I couldn't bear to lose Earth and River.

"Surely that can't be the reason," I said.

Lieneux shrugged, pursed her lips. "It really shouldn't fucking matter."

"You're right," I was a little too quick to say. "It shouldn't."

"You remember Naia, right?" she said. "I thought it was a cause worthy enough to go back in time. Wouldn't you think it was cause enough to go back in time?"

"I'd like to think so." Ythril bunched his eyebrows. "I don't know, actually."

"No," I said sadly. Meddling with the past is something we're rarely allowed to do, and the loss of Naia, much to my chagrin, did not qualify as an excuse. "But did you try to go anyway?"

"I found it in another universe."

I sat on the ground next to Ythril. Was the Naia I had just come from a fake? "No way."

"Fucking right? I found it all on my own!"

Ythril and I exchanged glances. We both had the same question.

"H-how does it fare?" I asked.

"Beautiful," Lieneux replied with a slight smile. "Perfectly safe."

I couldn't help but cry.

Ythril wrapped an arm around me. "Aw, Lux, you know better."

"No," I said, wiping away my tears. "Don't mind me."

"I found another Naia, and what's the thanks I get?"

"A cozy cell," Ythril replied. "It's hardly like prison at all."

Lieneux stomped her foot. "This place is hell!"

"Okay," said Ythril. "So then, why don't we leave?"

"You know this place is Thruszian-proof." Lieneux growled. "The guards let you in. And Sophie"—she paused, looking at me strangely— "Actually, how the hell did you get in here, past the guards? You ain't that damn stealthy."

I blinked. "What guards?"

"Oh, don't play dumb." Lieneux grabbed my wrist. "How the hell did you get in here?"

Ythril jumped up and eased Lienux's hand from my wrist. "Sophie's mind might be a bit fuzzy after that fire I was telling you about."

"Wait, wait, wait!" I exclaimed. "You and I need to talk about what happened back there, Ythril."

Lieneux wasn't ready to give up. "This place is fucking crawling with guards! What's your secret? Tell me so we can get the hell out of here."

"I don't know what you're talking about. What guards?"

I gripped the sides of my head and tried to slow my breathing. Was I going insane?

Ythril broke my thoughts. "What are you doing?"

"Trying," I said, "to keep from hyperventilating."

Lieneux scoffed. "Hyperventilating? What, you think you're human now or something?"

"I am human right now! I'm Evangelina!" I cried. Were they blind? Was I insane? What was this hell I'd found myself in?

"Look at that." Lieneux sighed. "This hellhole's so terrible, it drove Sophie batshit after only five minutes of being here. See now why I need to get the hell out of here?"

Ythril gingerly took my shoulders into his hands. "Whatever you did to sneak in here, we need you to do the same thing, so we can fly out of here. And maybe the three of us can return to Earth together, see how it's doing."

I started to say that I couldn't fly but decided not to waste my breath. Instead, I shrugged and shook my head, exhausted. Lieneux shoved by us to gaze outside her cell. Something invisible slammed her cell door shut in her face. Whatever it was, she yelled after it. "Fucking pigs!" So then, there were guards. Humans couldn't see them, and vice versa. I began to formulate a plan.

"I know how to break you out of here," I said.

Lieneux brightened up. "No shit."

"So you came to your senses." Ythril beamed. "Just in time. Visitation's almost up."

## III. Pacisci

How was I supposed to free Ythril and Lienux? After some reflection, I suggested that, since the guards could not see me, they probably wouldn't know what to do if I started dragging the two of them across the floor toward the exit (they'd have to float a little so that I wouldn't actually be dragging them). I suggested that maybe one would be limp and lifeless, while the other maybe protests and tries to break free. Ythril and Lieneux exchanged glances, the former grinning and the latter shaking her head.

"That's really stupid," she said.

I crossed my arms. "Do you have a better idea?"

Lieneaux only pursed her lips in response. Ythril patted her on the shoulder and said, "I'd trust my dear Sophie with my life. I don't believe we're in any real danger."

"Oh, of course not," Lieneaux snapped. "Because I suppose mind torture is no big deal."

I stared at her. "Mind torture? The punishment is that extreme?"

Mind torture is when our superiors force us into our mortal form—in our case, Earthlings—and engage in mental and physical torture, things that wouldn't work on hardy Thruszian bodies and minds but would essentially destroy our human selves. I'd seen it happen once. It was like a part of that Thruszian had died, and he was never quite right again.

"This better work, Soffialexinus, or I'm bringing you down with me."

I told them to stand far back in the shadows of the cell, so that when I opened the bars, the guards would think they were seeing things. At least, that's how I hoped it would work. I couldn't exactly see their reactions. So, I inched the cell bars open. For dramatic effect, I kicked the door the rest of the way open, causing some of the other Thruszians to jump in their cells. Near the entrance, another prisoner was being dragged in, but this halted, and he stared in my direction. I could tell he was trying to kneel, though the guards wouldn't let him, and he cried, "Look, whatever this is, I'll do anything. Anything but this place!"

The invisible guards forced him again to his cell. He continued. "No, I know what I saw! You saw it, too! If you let me go, I can prove it!"

I motioned Lieneux and Ythril to come up to the doorway and allow me to grab their collars. "Remember, float a little." Meanwhile, the words of the whiny Thruszian continued to echo throughout the room of cells.

"But I know what that was! If I handle it, would you let me go?"

Lieneux rolled her eyes. "What a pussy."

I scrunched up my face. I'd always hated that vile word. As we left the chamber, Ythril played dead, and Lieneux cursed and thrashed. I almost lost hold of her sometimes and had to tell her to tone it down a few notches. The whiny Thruszian pointed at us through his bars.

"Look, look! What can I do to make you believe me?"

Lieneux groaned. "Oh shit, here they come. Hurry up, Sophie."

I tried my best to increase my speed, but even though I wasn't pulling all their weight, they were still heavy. Something stopped us and yanked us back. When I turned around, I saw that a guard must have grabbed Ythril by the arm, but he was so committed to his role that he continued to play dead. His lifeless head lolled as he was yanked.

"Lieneux, I'm not strong enough for this!" I pleaded.

She sighed heavily and growled under her breath. "We're fucked."

Lieneux wrenched herself free from my grasp, appeared to combat her way through a few guards, and flew like light through the exit. I dropped Ythril, and he lay there, unresponsive. The heads of the other Thruszians stared on, all eyes on the exit, and I assumed the guards had dropped everything to seize Lieneux.

"Hey, human!" It was the whiny Thruszian. My heart pounded. It was the first time someone saw me as Evangelina. "Yes, you! I know what you're doing." I looked at him, wondering how he could see me for what I actually was.

"Look, let me out of here," he said, "and I won't turn you in."

"How can you see me as human?" I asked.

The whiny Thruszian smirked. Even in the dim light, I could tell he was bright blue, with an indigo horn curving like a scythe from his forehead. I was sure I'd known him at some point. Then I realized something. I looked around in all the cells and saw that all the Thruszian prisoners were humanoid. Ythril lay at my feet with his eyes still closed, so I crouched to whisper to him. "What exactly is this place?"

Ythril did not budge. I nudged him. "Ythril, get up. The guards are gone, and we need to be leaving soon. Plus, that noisy guy over there is onto me, somehow. Ythril!" I nudged him harder. Still no response.

"Let me out, and I'll help you," the whiny one cried.

"Shut up," I said. "There's nothing you can do to help me or yourself, so please do yourself and everyone else a favor, and shut up."

Mr. Whiney scowled at me, and I kept trying to wake Ythril. I couldn't leave him there. Although I didn't want to believe he'd be sentenced to mind torture, I didn't want to take any chances. So far, this place followed no recognizable logic. The whiney prisoner banged and banged on his cell bars, demanding I look at him. His voice was so loud and unwavering and tenacious, ringing through the large room and grinding on my ears.

"Look at me! Look at me! Look at me!"

I screamed, sticking my fingers into my ears. The whole prison shook with his echoing voice. When I finally did look up at him, he was right in front of me. Before I could react, he grabbed my shoulders and tapped his horn to my alicorn, leaning in until our foreheads were touching. I couldn't move, not because he was holding me too tightly but because I just *couldn't move*. My feet were stuck to the ground and I couldn't blink or speak. Every time I tried to scream, I could hear myself clearly in my head, though my mouth would not open lip from lip. From the ground, Ythril muttered softly, "I don't believe we're in any real danger."

"Look." My voice trembled. "Promise not to hurt my friend, and I'll try to help you escape."

His wide mouth curled into a most grotesque smile, as if he knew some big secret. "Atta girl." His hands tightened on my shoulders and he headbutted me.

At the moment of impact, I was sitting behind the bars of one of the cells. Confused, I examined my hands to make sure I was still Angie, which I was. Outside, the room of chambers was River's bedroom the way it looks when starlight pours in from the window, except it was the size of a football field. The bed was in the dead center of the room, and Ythril was sleeping in it. The whiney Thruszian was gone.

## IV. Exanimationes Incidamus

Not only was the whiney one gone, but all the other cells appeared empty now. I pushed and pulled at my bars, to no avail. I called to Ythril, and he stirred. Really, I had to wonder how he was able to sleep through all this. My banging and shouting and pulling at the bars did little more than cause him to turn over and bury himself deeper into the blankets. He seemed so far away, indefinitely unreachable. I stretched my arm through the bars and called his name one last time, and he groaned. Ythril propped himself up on his elbows and looked at me with sleepy eyes and his hair all tussled. Instead of the neat pastel rainbow that his hair usually is, all the colors and various locks looked smeared. Now that I think about it, his entire image was blurry.

"How did you actually doze off like that?" Thruszians don't sleep.

Ythril shrugged and got out of bed. "I don't know, but I think I should go help Lux."

"Help Lux?" I said. "She and the guards are long gone by now. They're probably giving her the mind torture as we speak."

"I'm sure she's fine."

"No, Ythril, none of this is fine. Please help me get out of here."

He started running toward the exit, waving to me. "Don't worry, Soph, I'll be right back. And Lux and I will bust you out of here."

"Wait, no! If they catch you, they'll...!"

Ythril had already taken off, soaring like a comet.

I sat back in my cell and tried not to let the utter silence freak me out. Somehow, I knew Ythril wasn't coming back. They'd catch him, put him through mind torture, and he'd never be the same. Meanwhile, I would rot in this cell. Once my human body died of starvation, I, or whatever remains of me, would be transferred back to the nebula to recuperate for who knows how long. Post-torture Ythril probably wouldn't recognize me once I was whole again, and River might have moved on. He would have worried himself sick, then, maybe, moved on. Actually, I wasn't sure what he'd do, but thinking about him made me cry; another thing about humans that I really cannot stand. It's inconvenient, and it makes me feel more vulnerable than I already am as a mortal.

Some find it bizarre that I'm willing to go through so much for mortality. I realize that. Some mortal beings wish to eliminate the end, whereas immortals like me actively seek it. So many billions of years are missing from my memory because who can fit it all? Not even Thruszian minds can handle so much. I've watched infant stars in their nurseries grow and thrive and die. I've seen galaxies collide. There have been so many promising planets, but it seems that the loveliest are always the most doomed, like Naia and Earth. Why was I assigned to Earth? For thousands of years, I've had to watch humans destroy and build and destroy and build, as if no one has learned anything.

I curled up in the shadows of my cell, hugging my legs close to my chest and sobbing into my knees. But Earth is such a beautiful planet. I can do more for it as a human than I can as a Thruszian, if that makes sense. Humans would take one look at me—a woman with glittery purple skin, hair the color of nebulas and galaxies, and the horn of what they refer to as a "unicorn" protruding from my head—and it doesn't take a genius to figure out that I'd be more trouble than help. I'd be an "alien," a "government conspiracy," the "enemy," a "hallucination," "the devil," and myriad more. I would be of so much more use as one of them. I would learn to love like them, which I believe I already have, and I would grow and age and die like them. I think it would be a beautiful end. It was a perfect plan, though I've yet to figure out how to fully give up my immortality. I often wondered if Evangelina would stay the same as River aged.

Of course, none of that mattered now. I was stuck in this forgotten cell. Remnants of Thruszian creation will continue to wander the universe, and occasionally, some will land on Earth. New demis would be born, though Earthlings are almost never involved in interplanetary conflict. Lucky them to have been born in the habitable zone of a safe solar system in a safe galaxy. Earth was perfect. Earth was *perfect*! I banged my fist against the wall and cried harder. It was a cruel, cruel thing to be assigned there and to know its beauty. I've known it and yearned for it, and now I will never have it. I was so close. And this wasn't the death I was supposed to have. There was nothing left to do now but lie down and await the gradual shutdown of Evangelina's body.

### V. Acceptatio

When I looked up from my knees and wiped my face dry, I saw that the scene outside my cell had changed again, but to what I could not tell. It looked dark with rays of light piercing through. I stood. As I walked closer to the cell door, I became increasingly aware that my chamber had become a rock floating through space. I watched as I slowly passed faraway worlds glimmering in the distance. I tried the bars, but they would not open. I tried to transform into Sophie, but that wouldn't work either. So, I sat cross-legged in my cell and let the vastness of space consume me. It pushed me along, immersing me in darkness and deafening silence. Faraway stars and galaxies ambled by. Asteroids floated indifferently in space. At least I'd have a nice view.

I wanted to try the bars again, but I knew they would never budge. So then. Just twenty or thirty more days, and Evangelina would be gone, only for Soffialexinus to reemerge and start all over again. There was no way for me to count the days, which I supposed would help me to zone out. I concentrated on the stars.

My wishes weren't meant to be, and as a being of the omniverse, I was more than acquainted with disappointment. I should have known better than to let myself get so upset, but in my defense, I was human. I had let my humanity get the better of me, which I suppose had always been my plan. And now my plan was thwarted. And so there I was.

Ythril appeared next to me, then. "There you are."

"Were you able to save Lieneux?"

"It's fine," he said. "She's safe."

I picked at my nails. "So, I guess you're trying to save me, too."

"I just thought I'd visit."

There was a period of silence.

"Ythril?" I said. "Have you ever wanted to be human?"

He laughed. "I guess. I mean, I can turn human whenever I want."

"No. I mean mortal. Have you ever wanted to be mortal?"

Ythril's smile faded, and he sat back, rubbing his neck as he considered my question. "Not really."

"I see."

"Why do you ask?" I told him my reasoning, and he nodded, saying, "I guess that makes sense. But I'd miss you."

"I'd miss you if the dead could miss," I said.

Ythril shrugged. "Maybe you could. Even if you were to die as a human, you were Thruszian at one point. So, I'm sure you'd come back in some way, shape, or form."

"But I just told you I wouldn't *want* to come back," I said. "And anyway, you'd be fine without me. You'd probably forget me after hundreds, thousands, or millions of years."

"You know better than that."

I sighed and ran my hand along the bars. "Am I being selfish, then?"

"I can't say for sure," Ythril said, putting his arm around me. "But if you find a way for that to happen, it's ultimately your choice."

I allowed myself to ruminate. My choice. My deliberate choice for an end, the only peace I could probably ever know.

"Maybe your consciousness will float through space forever," he said.

"Maybe."

"Is there any way I can convince you not to do this?"

I looked at him. "Probably not."

"What if there was a way for River to be immortal with you?"

Somehow, that irritated me. "That isn't what this is about! Not entirely, anyway. It's just a bonus, you know, to have someone to grow old with."

Ythril said nothing, but he grabbed my hand and held it. I continued, "Existing as a Thruszian is just that, existing. It's not *living* at all. What true memories do I have from these billions of years that don't end in some sort of colossal tragedy?"

"And so," he said, "you space-hopped."

"And so I space-hopped."

I waited for him to say something more, but his hand had disappeared from mine. He'd disappeared from my side completely. Solitarius iterum.

## VI. Excitatus

When I woke up, I was shocked to find myself back in bed, next to River, safe and sound. I stared at the ceiling with my hand on my thumping chest, trying to slow my breathing. I closed my eyes and counted backward from thirty, and I was fine. River, half-awake now from my stirring, nuzzled my neck and promptly fell back asleep.

And here I am now, sitting up and stroking his smooth, pale shoulder. My heart swells at his touch, at the sight of his sleeping face, and I wrap my arms around him, pulling him close to me. We've been together for a year and a half now. It's so funny that I've grown accustomed to measuring time using human units. In two hours, we'll be in the shower, and this bed will be empty; many of the little remnants of my dream will fade away with time. I've already forgotten bits and pieces of that dream. Two weeks ago, River caught a cold. Two weeks from now, I have a presentation due (which I plan to ace), which will help me along my path to graduation. And five years from now, I won't even remember what that presentation was about, but once that year comes, it won't even feel like five years have passed. In fact, the older one gets, the faster time seems to pass, making it all the more precious. Tempus fugit, sic transit gloria mundi. What I will remember throughout my life are the things that matter, which, I believe, grossly outweigh the tedious things, not in quantity, but in quality.

Though I won't be able to get back to sleep, I tuck myself back under the covers and cuddle up to River. I bury my face in his chest and run my fingers through his hair. River laughs sleepily and strokes the side of my face.

"What time is it?"

"6:06," I said.

His eyes open to groggy slits. "Why are you up so early?"

"I had a really vivid dream, and I can't stop thinking about it."

River blinks a few times before opening his eyes all the way and pressing his lips to my forehead. "A bad dream?"

"More like a *visionary* dream," I say.

He chuckles and closes his eyes again. "Visionary. I see. Want to talk about it?"

"There's not enough time."

"Two hours isn't enough time?"

"Actually, no," I say, slightly amused. In my head, I play with the concept of having enough time. It's not really something you can hold in your hands or keep in your pocket. Wouldn't it be nice to catch enough time and save it for later, for when you really need it? But no, you have to wait for it, and it takes at least some amount of planning. And by the time you have enough time, some of it has already passed. It starts with or without you. And anyway, I want to take my time with this, and I hate feeling rushed. The alarm would cut me off, and we'd have to continue discussing it another time, splitting my time into two separate slots, and by then, it wouldn't feel as natural. "No, it really isn't."

# About the Author

Jasmine was born in Toledo, Ohio on 5 July, 1992. She was *almost* born on the 4th of July, but life isn't always fair.

She received her BA in 2013 from The University of Toledo with a major in creative writing and a minor in Japanese. In 2015, she earned her MA in English literature from The University of Toledo as well.

"The Comet in the Sky," an early excerpt from *The Cosmic Adventures of Sophie Zetyld*, won second place in The Toledo Writers Workshop's 2015 "Find Your Inner Superhero" short story contest.

She currently lives in Ohio with her boyfriend and two mischievous cats, Tantan and Lulu (short for Lucrezia Borgia).

She enjoys ballroom dancing, ballet, video games (especially Soul Calibur, Super Smash Bros., Legend of Zelda, and Splatoon), j-fashion (especially Fairy Kei and Lolita), working out, reading, and, of course, writing.

CPSIA information can be obtained
at www.ICGtesting.com
Printed in the USA
BVHW080845170619
551189BV00002B/321/P

9 780578 457406